"Max!" Derm  through the do

He stopped short of the bed, breathless, his face drained of all color. "I heard from downstairs."

"And we're just fine," Jenna said. She was still rocking back and forth with Max in her arms, stroking his hair, holding onto him as tightly as he held her. He had quieted down, and seemed content to stay right where he was now. She was content to have him there, too. "He had a bad dream, but it's over now, and he's doing better—aren't you, Max?"

Max nodded, but didn't look up at his dad. His head was still tucked into Jenna's chest, and Jenna held him protectively, the way a mother would. To anyone looking on who didn't know Jenna might have been his mother, the way she comforted him. Dermott saw that. Saw that she had become a fierce protector of Max.

Now that her children have left home, **Dianne Drake** is finally finding the time to do some of the things she adores—gardening, cooking, reading, shopping for antiques. Her absolute passion in life, however, is adopting abandoned and abused animals. Right now Dianne and her husband Joel have a little menagerie of three dogs and two cats, but that's always subject to change. A former symphony orchestra member, Dianne now attends the symphony as a spectator several times a month and, when time permits, takes in an occasional football, basketball or hockey game.

Recent titles by the same author:

DR VELASCOS' UNEXPECTED BABY
THE WIFE HE'S BEEN WAITING FOR
A BOSS BEYOND COMPARE
ITALIAN DOCTOR, FULL-TIME FATHER

FOUND:
A MOTHER
FOR HIS SON

BY
DIANNE DRAKE

MILLS & BOON

All the characters in this book have no existence outside the imagination of the author, and have no relation whatsoever to anyone bearing the same name or names. They are not even distantly inspired by any individual known or unknown to the author, and all the incidents are pure invention.

First published in Great Britain 2009
Harlequin Mills & Boon Limited,
Eton House, 18-24 Paradise Road, Richmond, Surrey TW9 1SR

© Dianne Drake 2009

ISBN: 978 0 263 86868 5

Set in Times Roman 10¼ on 11½ pt
03-0909-58964

Harlequin Mills & Boon policy is to use papers that are natural, renewable and recyclable products and made from wood grown in sustainable forests. The logging and manufacturing process conform to the legal environmental regulations of the country of origin.

Printed and bound in Spain
by Litografia Rosés, S.A., Barcelona

FOUND:
A MOTHER
FOR HIS SON

CHAPTER ONE

"DERMOTT?" Jenna Lawson stopped half way into the elevator, blinked twice, then smiled. "Dermott Callahan? Is that really you?" Wow, he looked good. Better than she remembered, except he'd aged a little. Of course, it had been, what? Six years, or maybe closer to seven? Well, time had been kind to him. Very kind, except he had a distant look in his eyes, one that didn't fit the Dermott Callahan she remembered, and for a moment Jenna actually wondered if this was a case of mistaken identity. The Dermott she used to know couldn't have possibly looked as serious as this Dermott did.

But this Dermott spoke, and the voice was still the same. Deep, smooth, so sexy it was lethal. Yes, this was definitely Dermott. "Jenna. I'd heard you worked here. Wasn't sure that was still the case. But it's so nice bumping into you this way."

He gave her a long, intense stare, causing a tingle to work its way up her spine. Or maybe it was the memory of former tingles and that brief time when they'd been together. Nice time. Good memories.

By now the elevator was sounding a shrill warning to get out of the door, or else, so Jenna stepped inside and let it bang shut behind her. Except for one little old lady who kept her eyes glued to the punch buttons for each floor, she and Dermott were the only ones in the elevator, and yet he made no move to…to what? Hug her? Shake her hand? Be a little bit friendly? What was the proper protocol for two former lovers to meet again after so many years? "Technically, that *is* no longer the case. As of about ten minutes ago I'm a free woman, professionally speaking." As well as personally, but that was a long-standing, well thought-out condition.

Dermott arched his eyebrows, indicating mild interest, yet he didn't ask the obvious question most people would have, given what she'd just blurted out, and the silence between them in the elevator was almost deafening, it was so pervasive, as they moved slowly downward, from floor to floor. Even the old lady sharing the ride with them looked over to see if either one of them would take up the conversation.

"I was fired," Jenna finally supplied when he didn't ask, more to hear a human voice in what had turned into something akin to a vacuum. "Or, actually, prompted to find another position. That's what you get for…" No, she wasn't going to just blurt out that she'd talked her way out of her job. What was the point? It wasn't the first time, and probably wouldn't be the last.

"For what?" the old lady snapped. "For heaven's sake, don't leave us hanging this way. Tell us what happened."

Dermott arched his eyebrows again, and this time Jenna noticed a little sparkle under them. It was brief, but it had been there—the Dermott she used to know. The spark she'd loved. Although once, it had been permanent, not fleeting, like she'd just seen. So what was that about?

"For challenging the boss one too many times. She overworked the nursing staff, required that we work too many hours to make up for nursing shortages, which put patient care in jeopardy. I suggested she put her nursing uniform back on and come help us out on the floor and, well…" She shrugged.

Dermott finally cracked a smile. "You always did have a tendency to challenge authority."

"Only when it needs to be challenged. Today, that's what it needed."

"Good for you!" the old woman exclaimed. "You won't get anywhere in this world if you don't stand up for what you want."

Wise words, and so true. Jenna mulled them over as the woman marched her way out the door. "My supervisor wouldn't budge," Jenna said after the door shut. "And I was getting worried about medical mistakes. But nobody would listen to reason."

"As I recall, you have an unusual way of making your point heard," Dermott said.

"OK, so I tacked a nurse's uniform to her office door in case she'd forgotten what one looked like, and pinned a note on it inviting her to try it on for old times' sake."

"Now, that sounds just like you. Sassy!" Dermott laughed. "It's good to see you, Jenna. Good to know that your passion for your job is still just as…explosive."

Jenna laughed. "And you're just as blunt as you always were. So, are you still local? You haven't left Alberta to seek your fame and fortune somewhere else, have you?"

"Canadian through and through. Right now I'm in a little town north of Edmonton. No fame, definitely no fortune there, but it suits me."

"And you're married now, I heard?" It had happened quickly, if the rumors were correct. Four months after she'd ended their relationship, he'd gone off and gotten himself married.

There was a fraction of a pause before Dermott replied, "No. Not anymore."

Well, this was definitely awkward, Jenna decided as the elevator car came to a stop on the first floor and the doors opened. Positively a topic to avoid, if the scowl on his face had anything to do with the situation. Which, she believed, it must have. "But you're still practicing family medicine?" This seemed almost as awkward between them as it had been that day when they'd let their affair get out of hand and ended up in the unlocked supply closet. Dermott had been at the end of his residency, she'd been a fairly new nurse, and they'd had a few wonderful, intense weeks together that had scared her because with Dermott she'd lost reason and sense and all the cautions she counted on. That day in the supply closet, when the nursing supervisor had walked in and caught them, had proved it. No, they hadn't been fully engaged in the act, not even to the point of ripping off clothes. But it would have happened. Caution thrown to the wind ended it for them because what they'd had together back then had been so…out of control.

If there was something she never allowed for herself, it was any part of her personal life being out of control. What she'd done that day had scared her in ways she hadn't yet gotten over. Certainly hadn't ever repeated. One of the many foibles of being Jenna Lawson. "Well, take care of yourself, Dermott. It was nice seeing you again." Very nice. Very frightening because of all the feelings that came galloping back. Mostly, though, very nice.

"You too," he muttered, lagging behind, almost like he didn't want to be seen stepping off with her. "Look, um…Jenna," he said, before she got too far away. "I'm sorry about your job. You're a good nurse because you do care so much. Whatever happened, it's their loss."

Jenna spun around to face him. "It happens. Medicine can be harsh at times, and even harsher when you care. But I do, and I made my point. Admin listened, and they'll make the necessary changes here. And I'll survive somewhere else."

"I have a position open. Would you consider working in a small medical practice in a little town called Fort Dyott? Pay is poor, hours are lousy, accommodations are adequate, town is nice."

"That sounds like a real job offer." Truly a surprise. But was he serious about it? Because he'd asked with so little enthusiasm she wondered if he'd really asked or if she'd actually imagined it. If he *had* asked, this was so *not* like the Dermott she remembered it was almost eerie. Apparently, time hadn't been very kind to him. Since he was no longer married, was he reeling from a recent divorce, maybe? Or another life tragedy? She couldn't imagine it being his medicine because she'd never met anyone who loved the practice of it any more than Dermott had. Or one who had better natural instincts for it. "Is it, Dermott? Is it a job offer to come and work with you…a legitimate job offer?"

"Yes, I suppose it is. I need an office nurse. Someone I can depend on to be my second no matter what the situation, since I'm the only doctor in town. And you'll have to take calls when I'm not on duty, probably see some patients on your own… patients with minor complaints."

It sounded appealing, actually. But, again, spoken with no enthusiasm from him. That was odd. What intrigued her, though, was the small-town setting. It was a huge change from everything she'd done in the past, and all kinds of images popped into Jenna's mind—perfect little white cottages with white picket fences, tree-lined boulevards, city parks with lemonade stands. Suddenly, she was filled with nostalgia for a life she'd had a long, long time ago and chosen to throw away, and a stability she'd never known after she'd left her grandparents' home. "You're sure you're serious about this?" she asked, not wanting to raise too many hopes so quickly, not sure why she even wanted to hope. "Sure that you want me to come work with you?" It was crazy even considering Dermott's offer, but her heart was pounding a little harder, like she might really want the job. Or was all this merely a reaction to being fired a little while ago rather than really wanting Dermott's job?

Maybe, though, it was because he looked sad. And sad was something she knew so well.

"I had a medical assistant who went off and had a baby a few days ago, and she's not coming back, so it's a legitimate offer, Jenna. I don't have a lot to give you, like I said. My, um…my practice came on some hard times financially, so for a little while anyway, until I can get things back to normal, it might be a little tight. As part of your compensation, though, you'll have an apartment in the building where I operate the medical practice, if you want it. And your hours will be variable. It's a lovely area. Pretty. A little on the cold side in the winter, but not horrible." He shrugged. "There's not much more to say except the job is yours if you want it."

The job interested her, but the indicators weren't good here. Dermott wasn't Dermott, and that did worry her. Nursing jobs were easy to find. She had her graduate degree, for heaven's sake. She could command so much more than he was offering. On top of that, and in spite of her situation, she was going out into the world with a very good recommendation from the administration here. So what Dermott was offering her wasn't even close to what she could land for herself.

Then there was the obvious…their past relationship. They'd both moved on, both turned into different people. So could she work with him? Keep it professional, forget the past?

The truth be told, she didn't know, and that's what frightened her. She lived her life on a pretty straight line and Dermott had proved, once upon a time, that he could knock her off that line with so little effort.

Dermott came with risks she didn't want to take. Better to be safe, she finally decided. "I, um…I appreciate the offer, but right now—"

Before she could finish, he swept around her and, in the briefest moment, when their arms brushed, she felt a jolt shoot right through her—one like she'd never felt with anyone except Dermott. Immediately, she pulled back from him and crossed her arms.

"I understand, and it was nice seeing you again, Jenna." His voice was kind and, yes, a little sad. It was unmistakable, even after all these years. "I hope you find a job that suits you." That's all he said, then he walked away. The leather of his shoe soles clicked sharply across the marble in a precise rhythm, never breaking cadence.

Click…click…click… Jenna fixed on that cadence for a moment, trying not to fix on Dermott himself. But Dermott crept into her mind anyway. What had happened to him? Of all the people she'd ever known, he'd been the one who'd found so much joy in life—joy in the places no one would ever consider looking for it. He used to smile all the time. That had been part of his charm, one of the things she'd loved most about him.

But this man who walked away from her now—he marched like a soldier, rigid posture, straight shoulders. No real smile, maybe not for a long time judging from the deep set of his frown and the permanent creases in his forehead. So, what was his war? she wondered, and even worried as he pushed through the hospital's revolving door.

"Damn," Jenna muttered. She was tempted to run after him and accept the job, which was probably a huge mistake. She knew that, knew she shouldn't even entertain the notion. But it wasn't like she was following some major life plan, was it? Lord knew, she didn't follow life plans. Flitting in and out of jobs and relationships for so long, like she was only trying them on for size, was what she knew best, and the thought of taking on a real plan scared her. Yet helping an old friend for a while wasn't such a bad thing to do, really. Especially when that old friend looked so miserable.

It was Dermott's look that bothered her. Haunted her already.

The sound of unpleasant laughter broke through her muddled thoughts, and Jenna glanced away from the front door just as her ex-supervisor stepped off the elevator. Bianca Morrey, on the arm of her husband, was wearing her street clothes, and quite obviously leaving for the day while nurses under her supervision were overworked and overtired. One more nurse on the floor would have helped tremendously on the next shift, but Bianca didn't bend in that direction any more. The heck of it was, Jenna had been offered that supervisory position before Bianca, but she'd turned it down because she hadn't wanted to be that far away from patient care. That's where she was needed, and in a life with so little else going on, being needed was good. It was all she had.

And Dermott, a man with so many deep frown lines—he needed help. Her mind made up, Jenna raced after him to tell him she wanted the job after all.

Jenna? He'd asked Jenna to come work for him? And she'd actually agreed?

What the hell had he been thinking? Sure, he'd heard she was working at Stanton General when he'd sent in his papers for the refresher seminar on cardiac arrhythmias being held there, but he'd really had no intention of looking her up. Or had he? He hadn't gone on an exhaustive hunt through the various wards and wings, but he hadn't *not* looked when he'd walked up and down the various halls. Two days there without seeing her had convinced him that he was better off not seeing her at all, not seeking her out, then on his way out the door to go home, there she was. Just like it was meant to be.

OK, so maybe he'd hung around a little longer than he'd needed to after the seminar had ended, and walked a few more halls than was necessary. But to ask her to come and work with him in Fort Dyott? He hadn't meant to. The words had simply come out of him and it was like he'd been standing on the other side of the elevator listening to himself make a terrible mistake, unable to do anything about it. He liked Jenna, respected her abilities, but bringing her in would only complicate his already complicated mess of a life, and Jenna didn't always make things easy.

For five months now he'd done nothing but protect Max

from all the whispers and speculation, making sure that nothing bad touched his world again. It wasn't easy helping a little boy recover from the death of his mother, but that's just what he'd been doing, almost to the exclusion of everything else, including his medical practice, which he'd put on a part-time basis until he could figure out what came next. It was difficult, but he was dealing with it, and adding Jenna to the equation right now just wasn't a good idea because her complications would compound his. Truthfully, for the amount of work he had to offer, any other nurse or medical assistant would have been just fine. Jenna, though, was distracting, and Max still needed every bit of attention Dermott could give him. *Undivided* attention.

Max...curly blond hair, blue eyes with so much mischief in them. Damn, he loved his son. Max was the only good thing that had happened in his miserable six-year marriage, and it was truly amazing the way one totally unassuming little life had changed him in so many ways. But that's what had happened, and the only right thing to do in his situation was to protect his son. So, if Jenna worked out, that was good. A nurse like Jenna could help him get his medical practice back on track eventually, and that's what he really wanted to do when the time was right. Bar none, she was the best nurse he'd ever known and his remaining patients would love her. And if she didn't fit in...well, he couldn't imagine Jenna Lawson not fitting in anywhere.

That was, if she wanted to fit in. Jenna did have that disposition for not staying in any one place too long.

But if he kept his relationship professional with her this time, it could work out. And he had to keep it professional considering anything else would touch Max, which was something he would not allow. It wasn't like Jenna would ever hurt his son, because she wouldn't hurt *anyone* on purpose. She was the type who would, after a good hard rain, pick up an earthworm stranded on a sidewalk and put it back in the dirt. Max was vulnerable though…vulnerable to things Dermott didn't yet know or understand, and he had to be careful where Jenna was concerned because Jenna was so easy to become attached to. He knew that better than most. He also knew that she ran away, and that's what scared him about hiring her. If Max became too attached, and Jenna left…

No! He wouldn't let Max near that kind of pain. That's all there was to it. Being pragmatic about it, if he could be pragmatic about anything to do with Jenna, he would have to maintain a certain distance from her.

Of course, hadn't he vowed that once before?

Shutting his eyes, not sure whether to kick himself over his rash decision or give himself a congratulatory pat on the back, Dermott conjured up an image of the woman who had once come so close to being the love of his life. Honey blonde, shoulder-length hair, green eyes, a figure that made a man look twice or, in his case, a lot more than twice…

For his office she was the perfect choice, but in his life? Sure, he could tell himself that he just couldn't resist being around her again after so many years because, in part, that was the truth. Jenna was like unfinished business in a way. They'd been intense. Fast. So close to falling in love. Then nothing. The energy had been so strong, so addictive, and he needed that again. Of course, she could have changed. Settled down. People did. Just look at him, sitting here, having lunch with Max, with peanut butter smeared on his shirt. Who'd have ever thought this is what would make him happiest in the world, especially hating peanut butter the way he did?

But it did because he'd found something worth changing for. Had Jenna?

For her sake, he hoped she had. For his sake, though, he almost hoped she hadn't. Not too much, anyway.

"Where's she living?" the five-year-old asked. Grinning from ear to ear, with grape jelly all over that grin, he clutched a peanut butter and jelly sandwich in one hand and a cookie in the other, holding more tightly to the cookie.

"Upstairs. In the empty apartment." The one with absolutely no accommodations, and she was due here some time tomorrow.

Max scrunched up his nose. "It has spiders. Does the lady like spiders?"

"Probably not. So we'll have to get rid of them, won't we?" Dermott took a bite of his own peanut butter and jelly sandwich. Noon lunch with his boy had become the tradition, either here or at Frank and Irene's house, where Max spent his days. Barring any emergencies, he never broke the lunch date because it was one of the things he loved most about his life. "And we'll also have to give her some of the old furniture I put in Grandpa's barn after..." He stopped. It had been nearly five months now, and no one spoke of Nancy's death in front of Max. No exceptions. And someday, if and when Max asked about her, Dermott would deal with it then, doling out the truths as Max was able to deal with them.

So far, Max hadn't asked. Dermott was grateful for that, since his inquisitive little boy asked about everything else. "After the two of us moved in here. Grandpa said he'd help us do that later today, so I'll be counting on you to be in charge of getting that furniture put in the right place."

A deep frown popped up between Max's eyes, but he didn't say anything.

"What's that about?" Dermott asked, fighting to hold in a laugh. He knew that expression. Max was wrestling with a big decision.

"Grandma wants me to go with her for ice cream later on. She says it's very important, and I don't think she likes to go there alone."

"Very important?"

Max nodded solemnly. His frown deepened.

"Well, if it's very important, then you'd better go with her, don't you think so? Especially since Grandma doesn't like going alone."

A big grin broke out on Max's face and his eyes fairly twinkled. "I think so, big guy," he said, giving his dad the thumbs-up sign. Only Max's thumb was covered with grape jelly, which he spotted and licked right off.

Nancy had given him a beautiful child, and he owed her thanks for that. But for nothing else, because after she'd delivered Max into the world, she'd proceeded to make his own world a living hell. "Look, I think you need to go wash up and get ready to go back to Grandma's for the afternoon. Grandpa will be by to get you in a few minutes."

"Can't I stay with you, big guy? I won't get in the way if somebody comes in. Promise."

The truth was, he probably could. There weren't very many appointments scheduled. By design. Life had been tough for a while, and the people in Fort Dyott knew that his preference was to stay closer to his son these days. They respected it, and helped him do just that by seeking medical care in the Muledeer Clinic, which was in the next closest town to Fort Dyott. He knew, too, that so many people found that facing him was difficult, and painful, and that it was easier keeping a respectful distance for a while. However it was with them, they were good people. Nancy had been so beloved here that they'd overlooked her visible changes because that's just how they were and he knew there had to be guilty feelings. So he understood the avoidance issues some of them dealt with, and tried to let people know he held no hard feelings. With a few exceptions, it would all work itself out eventually. He was sure of it. "You know the deal. When I work, you stay with Grandma and Grandpa. But how about I come and get you early so we can go to the park and play ball for a little while before supper? Will that work for you?"

Max gave his head an affirmative nod. "Works for me, big guy."

Five minutes later, Dermott waved from the front stoop of his three-story red-brick building as Frank Allen drove away with Max. Frank and Irene adored the boy and, while they were Nancy's parents, they were the only ones he trusted with his son. They were good people. Good for Max. Surprisingly, good for him too. Perhaps because they'd seen some of the problems their daughter had, and understood some of the abuses she'd inflicted. *Some, not all.* The rest were Dermott's secrets to keep. Why hurt innocent people any deeper than they already hurt?

Dermott watched until Frank's truck disappeared around the corner, then returned to his office. Even though he practiced only about five hours a day right now, that seemed too much. Especially on a day after one of Max's nightmares, like today. Those were especially rough, the times when he wanted to be with his son, to hold him a little closer, a little longer.

But what he wanted wasn't always what he got.

Fort Dyott was larger than Jenna had expected. For some reason, she'd pictured a wide spot in the road, but there were several roads, actually. More than she could see in any direction. And there were shops, houses, churches, a movie theater—pretty much all the same things she was used to in Calgary, but on a smaller scale. By the time she'd reached Dermott's building, she'd decided she liked the looks of Fort Dyott. The people strolling up and down the streets appeared friendly. The streets were, indeed, tree-lined, and so far she'd come across two parks.

In fact, if she'd had a family to raise, this would have been an ideal place in which to do it. High praise, from a thirty-year-old who'd never imagined herself raising a family. Family implied direction and permanence and so far she'd successfully avoided that. Yet, if having a husband and children had been something she'd wanted to do, this would have been the right place in which to do it.

Fort Dyott seemed a nice little town with all the amenities, like where she'd been raised along the southern Alberta border. It was perfect here. Or would be perfect for a little while, until she got herself too involved and had to leave.

So maybe her brash, rash and otherwise impulsive decision to come here on Dermott's lukewarm invitation would turn out to be a good move after all. "No expectations," Jenna whispered, as she climbed out of her car and stared up at the old building. "Don't have expectations about this, and nothing will hurt you." That was a lesson she'd tried so hard to take to heart in the past, and always seemed to fail. No matter how hard she fought against them, expectations always found their way in, then ended up disappointing her.

Well, not this time! She knew what she was getting with Dermott. Or most of what she was getting. And hormones aside, she didn't need any more problems than she already had. Not even Dermott's problems, which did worry her. But she wasn't getting involved. Wasn't asking. Wasn't listening. Wasn't lending a shoulder or any other part of her body for anything. No causes, no crusades. No nothing, except work.

"So, just do it. Go up the steps and start over, Jenna." Easier said than done as those eight steps up to the front door were some of the longest, slowest steps she'd taken in a while. Of the three phone calls she'd had with Dermott since she'd chased him down the street and accepted his offer, only one had been even marginally friendly. And she wasn't sure that it was friendly so much as Dermott being relieved that she wasn't calling to change her mind about the job. Whatever had happened to him these past years wasn't good, and maybe that's what she dreaded the most—coming face to face with the thing that had sucked the spirit right out of one of the brightest, most lively people she'd ever met.

"But he's not the reason you're here," she lied to herself, as she laid her hand on the old glass doorknob, bit down hard on her bottom lip, and turned the handle. "It's about the job.

That's all. Just the job." Easy to say, but not easy to believe, and that's what frightened her. She could lie to herself all she wanted, but the lie wouldn't even hold up to a gentle breeze. Who was she kidding? All the firmest resolutions aside, she *was* here for Dermott. But as a friend? Or more?

Right now, she would fight, tooth and nail, to tell herself she was here just as a friend, and hope the other possibility didn't seep in. Although, even admitting there *was* another possibility gave her a deep-down queasy feeling right in the pit of her stomach. "Don't want that, don't want that…" she said, gritting her teeth. *"Do not want that."*

That was good. Now all she had to do was tell herself she was here for… For what? Peace of mind? Change of career direction? Simpler lifestyle? All good reasons, she decided. Good, and interchangeable. If she embraced her reasons hard enough, she'd believe them. Wouldn't she?

He's the reason you're here.

Damn it! Why couldn't she fool herself even for a moment?

Simple answer. She was here for Dermott, which scared her to death. So, she had two choices. Admit it, deal with it and, of course, not act on it. Or go and find another job somewhere else.

"You should have thought it over better," she admonished herself as she stood there, staring up at the building, wondering what would greet her on the other side of the door. Stupid thoughts! On the other side of that door were people who needed her. And a doctor who needed a nurse. If she could keep that in mind, she'd be good. "One step at a time, Jenna," she whispered, finally pushing open the door.

Jenna took her first step inside, plastering a perky smile to her face, ready to greet the patients as she walked through the waiting room for her first time, but after that one step her smile disappeared. The place was totally empty, the doorbell was jingling its merry tune to a completely hollow room. There wasn't even a waiting-room television tuned to an annoying cartoon channel blaring away. It didn't seem right, didn't seem normal, especially when Dermott was the only doctor in town.

"Hello," she called out tentatively, wondering if she should head down the hall to the exam rooms, or go back to her car, leave town and see if that clinic she'd passed in Muledeer a couple of hours ago needed a nurse. "Anybody here?"

There were noises above her, voices she thought, but she couldn't make them out. "Hello," she called, a little louder this time.

Again, no response.

"Dermott?" she called. "Dr. Callahan, are you here?" Her voice practically echoed, the place was so empty. "It's Jenna. I'm here."

Suddenly, there was a pounding on the stairs behind her, and before she could turn around to see who it was, a little boy practically threw himself at her feet.

"You must be the lady," he said, assuming a tough-guy posture—arms folded across his chest, face in a deadly serious, deadly cute scowl.

"And you must be Dr. Dermott Callahan," Jenna replied, fighting back a smile.

"Am not," he insisted.

"But that's the name on the door." To prove her point, she returned to the door, and showed the backwards outline of Dermott's name there. "See? It says 'Dr. Dermott Callahan, Family Practitioner'. So that means you must be Dr. Callahan." Pretty little boy, if boys could be called pretty. Lots of curly blond hair. Blue eyes. Beautiful eyes exactly like…Dermott's.

Dermott had a son? Why hadn't he mentioned it? "So, you are the doctor, aren't you?" she continued.

The little boy shook his head. "That's the big guy, he's the doctor. I just help out here when he needs me 'cos I'm too little to be a real doctor."

The child was just making her feel all warm and comfy inside, he was so adorable. "The big guy? Who's that?"

"He's my…" He scrunched his face a moment, thinking. "He's my big guy, and he's upstairs, getting the apartment ready for you. It has spiders, and I'll bet you hate spiders."

So Dermott was getting ready to stash her in a room with spiders. No romantic intentions there, which was a good thing. "So tell me, Dr. Dermott's son, what's your real name?"

"Dermott Maxwell Callahan." He nodded affirmatively, then added, *"Junior."*

"But you're not a doctor, Dermott Maxwell Callahan, Junior?"

He wrinkled his nose. "Call me Max. I'm going to be like Grandpa Frank when I grow up, and live on a ranch."

It was sounding like Dermott was part of a whole family system here. Ex-wife somewhere, child very much present, and parents or in-laws on a ranch. Tidy arrangement. One she almost envied. "I lived on a ranch for a little while when I was a girl. My grandfather's still there. He raises horses." They'd bred show horses, and a few that made it to the races. Riding those horses, and helping her grandfather…that's where she'd learned that life could be good. That's where she'd also learned to be afraid of too much of a good thing because good things didn't always last long enough.

"Can I ride one of his horses? All by myself? The big guy won't let me ride by myself. Neither will Grandpa Frank. But I promise I won't fall off."

"My grandfather has some pretty strict rules, too." Rules she should have obeyed, but hadn't. Rules she often wished she had obeyed, but didn't someone once say that you can't go home again? "You have to be at least this high before you can ride all by yourself." Jenna gestured a height that was a good two heads taller than Max. "But after you grow some, you come back and see me and we'll talk."

Max's response was a thumbs-up sign, and a big grin that

made Jenna grin right along with him. What a great little boy! How in the world could Dermott be so solemn and sad with someone like Max in his life? In some ways, Max reminded her of the way Dermott used to be. All smiles and optimism and enough charm to conquer the world. "Mind if I go find your father?"

Max pointed to the ceiling, as he scurried down a hallway leading away from the clinic. Jenna looked up, realizing he must have meant that Dermott was upstairs somewhere. So she climbed the first flight only to find herself standing on the threshold of what seemed to be a very nice apartment. No spiders visible, though, which meant she was probably one floor up from there. Next flight up she stopped at a spacious, surprisingly nice third-floor flat. And while she didn't exactly see the spiders, thanks to Max's suggestion, she did feel them. Figuratively speaking, of course.

"Dermott," she called out.

"Jenna?" He poked his head out from behind a stack of boxes. "I didn't expect you until tomorrow."

"I got an early start," she said, surveying what was going to be her home. "There was nothing to keep me in Calgary."

"It's better than it looks." Dermott laughed, stepping out into full view, wiping his dirty hands on the back of his jeans. "The apartment...it has what real estate agents would call potential."

She'd thought the same thing about Dermott, once upon a time.

"Although I think the potential might have been a little cleaner tomorrow," he continued.

Even in the dark, covered with cobwebs, Dermott was gorgeous. But he was divorced, or in the middle of a divorce, she had to remind herself. All looking, no touching. That was the rule. But, dear lord, he was good to look at. She'd always admired that about him. Couldn't help herself then, couldn't help herself now.

It was a brief admiring look, she told herself. Just a tiny little one that didn't count. One quick glance and it was out of her mind. Gone. Vanished. Poof! "But I don't have to pay extra for the spiders, do I?"

He chuckled. "You must have met Max. He's a little obsessed with the eight-legged creatures right now but, I promise you, there are no spiders here."

"Cute little boy. Smart."

"Thanks. I'm a little partial, but I think so, too."

"You never mentioned him when we talked. Why's that?"

"I don't generally. Max and I keep to ourselves most of the time. We, um…we keep our lives pretty private, pretty simple."

Well, this was awkward. No two ways about it, she'd stumbled into a situation where she wasn't wanted, and from there she didn't know which way to go. So she didn't. She kept quiet, stood still and waited for Dermott to make the next move.

Which he did after he'd felt the long, sticky pause between them. "OK, let's just get this out of the way," he said, before the next second of awkward time had passed between them. "I'm a widower. Almost five months now."

"Oh, Dermott! I didn't know. I'm so sorry. It must have been so difficult for you and Max. And he's so young. Have you two—?"

Dermott shook his head, effectively cutting her off. "I never, *ever* talk about it around Max. Nobody else does either. Understood?"

He'd just put her in her place, good and proper. That's what she understood. Another thing she understood was that this was not the same man she'd nearly loved all those years ago. He was gone and in his place stood someone she wasn't sure she even liked very much. The old Dermott had been kind and open. This one was cold, and evasive. The old Dermott had been very generous with the truth. This one withheld it.

Yes, that's what she understood, and it's also what she had to remember. They'd both changed. Times were different. It was probably for the best because now she could put aside all those silly notions and memories.

But, darn, he was still gorgeous. That hadn't changed.

CHAPTER TWO

WELL, it wasn't a grand welcome, yet here she was, five hours after arrival, making plans. Real plans. New curtains, a coat of yellow paint in the kitchen to brighten it up, a nice floor lamp and an overstuffed chair. Just like she had a right to make plans here. But she couldn't help it. For once, she so wanted something to work out, wanted her roots to plant themselves deep enough to keep her here for a while.

For someone who'd promised herself no expectations, she sure had developed her fair share awfully quickly. It was a worry, but right now she didn't want to think about it. She had throw rugs on her mind, and pictures for the walls. Nice things she didn't usually allow herself.

Because she was tired. That's what she was telling herself. She was a little out of kilter because she was tired. She'd had a long trip getting here, lots of jitters over her decision, and even more jitters over seeing Dermott again. Put them all together and they resulted in silly thoughts. Tomorrow she'd be rested, and thinking straight again. Yes, her resolve would be back where it should be, and her life would get back on the track she'd designated.

At least, that's what she was telling herself now. In the meantime, she was undecided about what clothes to unpack for the night, and what to leave alone. Staring into her open suitcases, Jenna was on the verge of simply shutting the lids and letting it all go until tomorrow when a buzzer from the first floor sounded. One buzz, then a couple more frantic buzzes coming from the clinic door. An emergency? The clinic had been empty all afternoon, but now somebody was in need, when Dermott wasn't here?

Dashing down the rest of the stairs, Jenna ran straight to the door, then opened it, to be greeted by a big man with a small, bloody towel wrapped around his arm. "Saw Doc and Max having ice cream downtown, and didn't want to bother them. But I heard he had a new nurse working here, so I figured I could let you have a look at this." With that, he held out his arm, but didn't remove the bloody towel.

"I can call Dermott. He gave me his cellphone number, and—"

"No, ma'am. That won't be necessary. It's just a little scratch, and it would be a shame to interrupt his time with the boy just to take care of it. You *are* the new nurse, aren't you?"

Jenna nodded. The new nurse who was a little perplexed by this.

"Then it's *you* I'm here to see." That said, and quite emphatically, he stepped all the way inside and shut the front door behind him. "No sense in driving all the way over to Muledeer for the doc over there to take care of this when you can do it. It's a good two hours away, and I'd just as soon get this patched up here and get on home and go to bed."

Muledeer? Why would he drive all the way there when Dermott was right here? That made no sense at all. "What happened to you arm, Mr....?"

"Wilkerson. Isaiah Wilkerson. And I'd extend a hand to greet you, ma'am, but I put my shaking hand through a plate-glass window about fifteen minutes ago. Tripped myself going up a ladder to hang a picture, and used the window to break my fall." He finally unwrapped the towel, showing Jenna what turned out to be a pretty nasty gash. One that would need stitches, and maybe a whole lot more, depending on the extent of any tissue damage he'd caused himself.

"Are you light-headed, feeling nauseated, woozy, Mr. Wilkerson?"

"Only when I look at the blood, ma'am." He did look down at his arm, then turned his head away.

"Are you here by yourself? Or did someone else drive you?"

"By myself. My wife's off visiting her sister tonight, and instead of bothering her to come bring me here, I drove myself. I am feeling a little tired, though. It's…coming on me right now. A…groggy…feeling…"

So was the deathly pallor washing down over his face. His speech was slowing and slurring, too, and Jenna knew this great hulk of a man was about to go out on her. "Look, let's get you to the exam room, where you can lie down." She hadn't even seen the exam rooms yet. "After that we'll figure out what needs to be done."

"Appreciate that, ma'am." He sighed heavily, struggling to keep himself upright.

"Jenna," she said, grasping him tightly around the waist as his knees started to dip. "Any man I have to carry like this gets to call me by my first name."

"Jenna," he said, straining to stay upright now. "Pretty name. Got a daughter…name's Jennifer. Is Jenna short for…?"

The interminably long trip down the hall to the exam rooms ended at the first room, where Jenna pushed open the door with her foot and was thankful to see an exam table not more than five steps ahead of her. Mr. Wilkerson had turned into deadweight, and while Jenna was up to hefting a pretty large man, Isaiah Wilkerson was larger than the average, and every bit of him was rock-hard muscle. "It's Jenna. Jenna Joann Lawson."

"Pleased to…make…your acquaintance, Jenna," Isaiah grunted as he dropped down onto the hard surface of the exam table and immediately plopped down onto his back.

Jenna sprang around the table to crank up the head, then she turned on the overhead light. "Look, I really need to call the doctor," she told him as she scurried to assess the various medical supplies in the room. It was a nice, tidy little exam room. The equipment was outdated, but still very functional, and it put her in the mind of something from the 1960s. It probably was, come to think of it. Dermott had, most likely, acquired the practice, as well as the equipment, from its original owner. Wooden exam table, not chrome or steel. Wooden cabinet. Old-fashioned sink. Overall, it had a nice, homey feel to it, and she liked it.

"No doctor! Like I told you before, I don't want…to interrupt him when he's out with the boy. They need…their time together," Isaiah said, his voice growing weaker. "If you think I need a doctor…all that bad, I'll drive myself…over to Muledeer."

Now, that was just plain crazy. "You won't make it to Muledeer," she said, laying a gentle hand on the man's shoulder as he tried to sit up. "You won't even make it to the front door."

"I'm the patient here. Don't I have…some rights? Some say…in who treats me?" His voice finally trailed off to a whisper and Jenna took his pulse to make sure nothing besides the obvious was going on. It was strong. His respirations were good, too. A little shallow, but not alarmingly so.

And, yes, he did have a say in who treated him. But in his current condition, in a one-doctor town, those rights didn't mean much. "Look, Isaiah, the first thing I need you to do is trust me. OK? You've lost a lot of blood and I don't want you passing out, but that's what's going to happen if you don't take it easy. So lie back, close your eyes, concentrate on breathing, and I'll take a good look at your cut. If I can treat it, I will. But if it requires a doctor…"

"Do your…best… Don't interrupt…"

"I know. Don't interrupt Dr. Callahan." Stubborn, *stubborn* man. Well, she'd just have to be more stubborn than he was.

"Like I said, trust me, Isaiah." She completely removed the towel from his arm. "I've been a nurse for quite a while now, and I know what I'm doing."

She also knew his cut was so deep that it required stitches. Which she could do, but wouldn't. It wasn't her place since the doctor was only a few blocks away. "Isaiah, I want you to rest here for a few minutes, will you? Since I'm new, I don't know where the supplies are, and I've got to go on a little hunt for a few items. You're not bleeding right now, so I want you to stay still. And relax." He needed a sedative, and a painkiller, which she couldn't prescribe, so that gave her even more cause to call Dermott. Even if it was against her patient's will.

"I'm not going to lose my arm, or anything like that, am I?" he choked out.

"Good heavens, no. You're going to get some stitches, but that's about the worst of it." As a precaution, before she left the room, Jenna took his blood pressure, and wasn't surprised that it was low, but not critically. With all his bleeding, hypotension was bound to happen. "Just rest. I'll be back in a few minutes," she said, then ducked out of the exam room.

One her way to find a supply closet, she dialed Dermott's phone. It rang twice, and when he picked up, rather than saying hello, he led off with, "Care to join us for ice cream? Wasn't peppermint your favorite flavor?"

He remembered that? Had he ever even seen her eat ice cream?

"Dermott, I'm with Isaiah Wilkerson. He put his hand through a window, and he doesn't want me calling you."

Dermott cleared his throat. "How bad is it?"

"Not critical, but pretty bad. He has a four-inch gash in his right forearm, about three inches above his wrist, that will need stitches. And he's threatening to go to a doctor in Muledeer if I call you in to take care of him. I mean, he *really* doesn't want you."

"I'll be there in ten minutes, but don't tell him I'm coming because he absolutely *will* walk out if there's any way he can do it. And in the meantime, go ahead and stick in an IV for me. He probably needs his fluid volume pumped up some. Use Ringer's for now, since he's been bleeding, and add about 5 of Valium to relax him…and keep him down on the table. IV bags are in the gray supply cabinet, top shelf. The Valium is in the locked medicine cabinet in my office. The key is in my office wall safe, and the combination is…" He paused for a moment, then went on, "Eleven-fourteen. And if you have time, get him cleaned up and prepped for me. Isaiah's a big complainer, by the way." He chuckled. "Nice man, but squeamish when it comes to doctors."

Eleven-fourteen. That was her birthday. November fourteenth. Maybe he'd known about her ice cream preferences, but surely this was a coincidence. Dermott couldn't have known when her birthday was. Could he? She thought about it for a moment, and shook off the notion of it being anything more than a coincidence. His safe combination was merely happenstance. That's all!

Ten minutes later, true to his word, Dermott was there, standing in the hall outside the exam room, looking in while Jenna finished anchoring the IV and injecting the Valium into it. Before he could speak, Jenna raised her finger to her lips, warning him to be quiet. Then she gestured to the furthest end of the hall for their rendezvous, and met him there a minute later, after she'd put an extra sheet over her patient. "Bleeding's stopped, blood pressure's low—ninety over sixty-five—pulse and respirations normal. And the last thing he told me before he nodded off was that I was not to call you. So, what's that all about, Dermott? He claimed he didn't want to interrupt you from having ice cream with Max, which might be true, except he threatened to drive for two hours to find another doctor, and that's just absurd."

"People here don't want to disturb me. After my wife died I cut back on my hours so I'd have more time with Max. People here respect that, and try to help me do it. That's all it is. Nothing devious. Nothing secretive. They just want to help me."

"Maybe. Although making a trip to Muledeer when you're in Mr. Wilkerson's condition still doesn't make any sense." It would be nice to think that people could be that caring, though.

Dermott shrugged, but didn't respond. "Is the wound clean, or jagged?"

Apparently, the topic was closed, if not in discussion then most certainly in the body language Dermott was putting up. Stiff shoulders, deep scowl, impatient eyes. Secretive or not, it was strange. "Good, clean edges. Looks like one slice."

"Any tissue compromise that you could see?"

"No, and his sensory perceptions are intact. Good feeling all the way around."

"Anything out of the ordinary?"

Except the doctor? Or the stubborn patient? "Do you really want me to tell you what's out of the ordinary here, Dermott? Because I'd be happy to."

Dermott leaned in, smiling. "One of the things I always liked most about you, JJ, was your feistiness. You always did speak your mind, even when no one wanted to hear it. In fact, isn't that what got you here?"

"Believe me, Dermott. This isn't feisty. Whether or not you want to hear this, I'm curious and a little angry that a man with a serious condition might have killed himself because he didn't want to interrupt his doctor's trip to the ice-cream parlor. And I'm concerned that the doctor's not more concerned than I am."

"Oh, I'm concerned. But I can't control the people in Fort Dyott. They're going to do what they want to do and I have to respect that. This is small-town medicine and it comes with rules you're not used to."

"Rule number one, no matter where you are, is to save your patient, Dermott. But your patient seems to think it would be an imposition on the doctor." OK, so she wasn't ready to give up on it. She was stubborn. She admitted it. And she wanted to know, darn it!

"You always were a fierce advocate, Jenna. That's what makes you such a good nurse."

He used to be a fierce advocate, too. So what had happened to change that in him? "Your equipment is at Isaiah's bedside. I've got portable oxygen standing by, just in case, and he's sedated. I've also got an antibiotic ready." All the things a good surgical nurse would do, and she was a good surgical nurse. Also a perplexed one. "So you're ready to go, any time you want to start." Jenna handed Dermott his magnifying goggles, then stepped back and folded her arms across her chest.

Dermott let out a low whistle. "Feisty and stubborn. It's aged well on you, Jenna. Better than I could have hoped for."

"What's that supposed to mean?"

"It means you haven't changed a bit. And I still like it!"

"So, how's he doing?" Jenna asked.

"The sedative has him settled in for a little while. I left a message for his wife to come get him, and told her there's no hurry. That he's fine, and snoring away like a broken chainsaw."

"You did a good job, Dermott." It had been nice watching him work again, even for something relatively simple.

"Just a few stitches. You could have done them yourself."

"I don't overstep my job. There was a physician on call, so it wasn't my place to do that." Jenna dropped down onto the brown leather couch across from Dermott's desk and knew right off she could spend the night there, it was so comfortable. It was a nice office. Rugged, manly. Something that suited him. "So let me get something straight. You do take emergency calls when you're away from the office, don't you? You don't really make people go all the way over to Muledeer?"

"Of course I don't. I'm on call around the clock."

"Even though the people here don't want to bother you with their emergencies?"

"Believe me, most people will bother me. You'll find out soon enough. But Isaiah…he's his own special breed of ornery. Nice man who has a real soft spot for children, and he didn't want to interrupt my evening out with Max. Like I told you before, that's all it is, Jenna. Don't read more into it than that."

Maybe that was the case, but Dermott was visibly uncomfortable with this discussion. She knew his body language, and the tight way he held himself and twisted away from her was practically screaming that he didn't want to discuss this. So she wouldn't. There was something more here, but she was the outsider and it was quite clear, even with Dermott, that she wasn't going to be let in. So she scooted herself to the edge of the couch and pushed herself up. "I'd like to be friends again, Dermott."

"We are friends," he said.

"Are we?"

"What gives you the idea that we're not?"

So many things did, but she wasn't in the mood to deal with that now. Maybe the professional approach was best. Keeping her distance certainly wouldn't get her into any trouble and, for once, that was probably a good idea. "Look, I'm going to go sit with Mr. Wilkerson until his wife comes to get him." And try not to think about anything. Including Dermott. Including this whole, peculiar situation about his medical practice.

Jenna discovered a tin of tea-bags in her little pantry, and that's all she needed. She wasn't sleepy, wasn't even hungry now, although she hadn't eaten for a while. Tea was enough, however, so she filled the teakettle and sat it on the stove top, then plopped down in the old chair in the corner, still trying not to think about anything. Especially not about Dermott. She didn't want to pass judgment on anything so early into their professional relationship, although she was afraid his ill-sorted state of affairs here was already clouding her judgment a bit.

She did want to fight her way through her skepticism, though, and keep an open mind. Meaning she wasn't making any firm decisions yet. Because she did want this to work for her. For once, a little stability sounded good. So did staying in a place she didn't consider a temporary stopover on her way to the next temporary stopover. It was like she lived her life from moment to moment, and that's all there was, a string of unrelated moments. But now that she was here, she seemed to want connection in a way she'd never wanted it before, even though she was afraid of it.

As the tea kettle began whistling, Jenna listened to the shrill pitch of it, actually savoring the way it drilled right through her brain. She'd been in such a fog lately. Sometimes it felt like her entire life was all foggy. Yet she always wanted to believe there was something more, something better. Something clear and bright ahead for her.

Right now she was pinning some hope on Dermott being clear and bright, and she wasn't quite ready to give up on it. They'd been great together once. Physician and nurse working beautifully alongside each other on the job on the one hand. Man and woman relating beautifully outside the job on the other. Neither of those relationships had been explored thoroughly enough to draw any conclusions, though, which was a regret that had come to mind so many times over the years. They'd had their fling, spent a few lovely nights... It had been on the verge of a relationship, she'd give it that much. But that's all it had been—on the verge. Because that's all she'd allowed. All she'd wanted.

Well, it was on the verge again, but not personally this time, as she was older, wiser. Much more experienced. Yet, as discouraged as she was over the prospects of Dermott's medical practice merely fizzling out from a lack of activity, which would put her right back on the road to the next temporary stop, she wasn't going to give up on it. In fact, to prove to herself that this arrangement could work, maybe she'd go ahead and unpack her undies after she had her tea. Yes, that's exactly what she'd do. Unpack her undies, move in fully. It was symbolic of hope, wasn't it? Or of committing herself to something more than temporary.

Permanence. It had a nice feel to it. Worried her. Caused a little panic, too, just thinking about it. But it's what she so desperately wanted, even though she didn't know how to get it for herself. Hadn't wanted to, because permanence wasn't permanent. "Permanence," she whispered. Then whispered it a second and third time to see how it felt.

If felt rickety. She wasn't sure she could trust it. How many times before had she convinced herself she was in the right situation only to find out she wasn't? Permanence. Not to be trusted, she decided. But this time?

Time would tell, she supposed.

Forcing herself to shake off her glum mood, Jenna pulled herself out of the chair, and plodded into the kitchen to silence the screeching kettle and fix a cup of tea. She was on her way back to the chair with a steaming mug of cinnamon-flavored tea when a muffled knock at her door startled her.

"Jenna," Dermott called, before she got there. "Can we talk?"

"About the job?" she asked, as she opened the door to him. She hoped so, because she wasn't ready for any personal unveilings, revelations or confessions tonight. Especially when her undies were still packed away, their status yet to be determined.

"About us."

"There isn't an us, Dermott. That was a long time ago, and it didn't go far enough to be considered anything other than a good time between two people who got along. We weren't headed anywhere then." He didn't come inside. In fact, when she opened the door he stepped back and leaned against the staircase railing. It was a casual stance, arms folded across his chest, one leg crossed over the other. Casual, and utterly sexy.

Dermott chuckled. "You have your version, I have mine. And for my version, I have a couple of things for which I'd like to apologize."

"Why?" she asked, trying to muster up a little indifference when her heart was doing the exact opposite. This was the way he'd affected her all those years ago, and nothing had changed, it seemed.

"I remembered some nice times between us, and I haven't had much of anything nice in my life lately. Other than Max, that is. I thought having you come here would…" He shifted position, crammed his hands into his jeans pockets. "You're too good to be stuck in a practice like this one, and that's my first apology. I knew that when I asked you here, but I asked you anyway because I always liked having you around. We were good together. You made me a better doctor, and that's something I've remembered all these years. So when I saw you, and you said you were looking for a new position…"

So the *us* he wanted to talk about was professional. That was disappointing. Safe, but disappointing. "I'm the one who came running after you, remember? You offered, I declined, then changed my mind. So there's no need to apologize, because it *was* my choice. And I liked working with you, too." Better than she had with any other doctor, actually.

"You did?"

"I did. You were…different. So many of the other doctors took the nurses for granted, and you… It was like we were equals. You respected us. Gave us credit for what we knew. And you weren't put off by suggestions, like so many doctors are."

"Because we're all in it together. It would be stupid not to respect someone with a different kind of experience than mine because I never know what's going to click medically with a patient. As far as I'm concerned, every opinion counts, especially when they're coming from a nurse who has such a good instinct for her work. To be honest, Jenna, I'd have rather had you, a nurse, at my side than just about any *doctor*, and it wasn't because you're beautiful and I enjoyed looking at you. I enjoyed your professional approach, trusted it, trusted you."

She didn't know what to make of that because he'd never said such things in the past, but she was pleased. Surprised, and pleased. He knew her favorite ice cream, thought she was a competent professional, thought she was beautiful…so much awareness and she wasn't sure she wanted anyone to be aware. It almost caused her some hope…hope for other things, things she was afraid to let in. "I'm sorry your times haven't been so good lately, Dermott. I know it must be difficult raising your son alone, and…" Did he still think her beautiful? "Did you remember my birthday?"

He cleared his throat. "Your birthday?"

"November fourteenth. You know, eleven-fourteen."

"What makes you think I would remember your birthday?"

"It's the combination to your safe. I just thought…" Whatever she'd thought was crazy. And now the moment was on the verge of turning awkward. She could feel it, and from the strained expression on Dermott's face, and the way he was standing straight and stiff now, he could feel it, too. Time to change the subject, find a graceful way to turn around the conversation before any more silly questions popped out. "Anyway, I'm glad I decided to come here. It seems like a nice place to live, and—"

"She was a drug addict. My wife. She abused drugs and alcohol and did bad things. It was the talk of the town before she died, still is at times. And I thought you should know because you'll hear it from other people at some point. I was married to a woman who had serious problems that weren't kept very quiet, or very private."

"Oh, my…" That explained so much, and her heart did go out to him. But he wasn't here looking for sympathy, wasn't looking for someone to talk to. He was merely here to state a fact, and that's how she had to take it—as a matter of fact. "I appreciate your honesty. It couldn't have been easy for you."

"It wasn't. Not for either of us." That's all he said. Then he turned to leave.

"So what's the other thing you came to apologize for?" she asked, not sure if she wanted to change the tone of his parting, or if she wanted to keep him there a while longer. "You did say there were a couple of things."

He stopped, still facing away from her, then paused, as if considering whether or not he wanted to get into anything else with her, or if one truth was enough to admit. Then, finally, he turned back to face her. "Well, there *was* that brief but unforgettable few weeks we had…culminating with that day in the closet." His mouth curved into a wicked smile, one that had never failed to pull her in.

"And you want to apologize for that? Because I thought it was rather good."

"I want to apologize for it not being more than a few weeks. And *I* thought it was more than *rather* good."

Those were memories that had always brought about a wistful sigh, followed by some very pleasant fantasies. And she, too, was sorry that those few weeks couldn't have been followed by a few more. "It was what it was." Lame words, because there could have been more, but she'd used their little escapade in the closet to end everything after she'd got scared by the intensity of her own feelings. "No apologies necessary."

"So are we OK about this, Jenna? You and me working together in a practice that isn't exactly thriving these days?"

Was this where he came right out and told her he wasn't interested in anything other than work? Because that would be for the best. Getting the relationship on track right now so there would be no misunderstandings later on was exactly what they needed to do. Although it was a little disappointing. "I'm OK about it."

"But you're bigger than life, Jenna. I saw that the first time I set eyes on you and I doubt you've changed all that much.

You tackle life in a way no one else does, and I'm not sure anything I have here will suit you for very long."

"You underestimate me, then."

"I don't underestimate you, Jenna. Trust me, that's something I'd never do."

She was flattered. But afraid of the look she saw in his eyes. This was the Dermott she used to know, but in such a different way. It was something intense, and profound. "I want to stay here, Dermott. Although the work does have to fulfill me, and I am concerned that if you're cutting back on what you do there won't be enough for me to do here. I'm not larger than life, and I try not to have big expectations, but my work…it's all I have, and what I'm seeing here scares me, because you don't have the same passion for it the way you used to."

"The passion hasn't died, Jenna. But the circumstances have changed, and I do have different priorities now. Max comes first in everything, and that's the only way it can be. I've cut back my practice because I have to. With help, I can start growing the practice again, and it's time to do that. But my work won't consume me the way it did when you used to know me because I have Max now."

She understood that, and even envied him his newfound conviction. But that didn't alleviate all her doubts over how this could work out. Or if it would. Maybe there *was* an expectation creeping in, even after she'd tried so hard to keep it out. Damn it, though. This was Dermott. How could she not have expectations of some kind? Dangerous, if not deluded expectations? "One day at a time, Dermott. Maybe that's the way we should start this. We'll keep the expectations to a minimum and simply take it as it comes. OK?" No expectations? Yeah, right! Still, maybe unpacking only *half* her undies would be the smartest thing to do.

"Slow and careful," he agreed.

She nodded. "After my last job, I'm ready to be someplace

less complicated. Someplace where the people are nice. Who knows? Maybe I can get used to the less encumbered lifestyle and find that it suits me after all."

"Less complicated?" He chuckled bitterly. "If that's what you're looking for, you've come to the wrong place because everything here is complicated, in a lot of different directions."

"Not if the complications aren't from one of *my* messes, it's not." She laughed, but it was a disheartened laugh. "I don't always blurt out my frustrations to people in the elevator, but that had been a really horrible day, one of the worst in my life, and it was either blurt or kick the wall. And, trust me, with the way I was feeling I probably wouldn't have even noticed a few broken toes."

"That bad?"

"That stupid. I knew Admin wouldn't change their attitudes for me, but that didn't stop me from barging in where I wasn't invited. They had to know how their policies affected patient care and, more than that, patient safety. I'd also talked to a reporter…"

Dermott laughed out loud. "Of course you did. Anything else wouldn't have been pure Jenna Lawson. Any regrets for what you did?"

She shook her head. "They're looking to hire a few more nurses now, make some administrative changes, and that's good. So, do you want to come in for some tea? I just fixed a pot."

"Cinnamon."

Actually, it *was* cinnamon she'd found in the cupboard, wasn't it? She hadn't thought much about it, but cinnamon was her favorite, and probably not the most common thing to stock in a pantry where there was little else. "You remembered that, too?" Unless this was a coincidence like her birthday, she was flattered again. Ice cream, birth date, *and* favorite tea…

"What I remembered was that night after work, when five

or six of us went to the café. You ordered cinnamon tea, and I think it was the first time I ever knew that tea came in any flavor but plain. You opened a new world for me that night."

"So you like cinnamon tea now?" She recalled that night. He hadn't been particularly fond of the tea after she'd convinced him to order it, and after several tastes, he'd finally traded it for a cup of coffee. Black. Plain.

"No. I still like my coffee."

Jenna laughed. "So what new world was it that I opened?"

"If you recall, I was the only guy in the café drinking regular coffee, and that's sort of been the lot of my life since then. People like their lattes and cappuccinos and espressos, and all those chocolate-caramel-vanilla-hazelnut-amaretto flavors in their coffees, and when you step up and order your coffee plain and black, you get a funny look from a lot of people. They practically beg you to order what they have, to be like they are, to fit into their mold or stereotype. *Just one sip, you're really going to love it.* Well, I was trying my hardest to impress a pretty girl that night by drinking her hideous cinnamon tea but what I discovered was that sometimes putting on airs is too tough. In the end, depending on how it works out, you end up sentencing yourself to a lifetime of cinnamon you hate, or somewhere in the future you'll have to admit that you were lying, which could make people wonder what else you lied about since little lies, like cinnamon tea, usually snowball. The world that opened up to me over a plain, black coffee is that it's always best to be honest about who you are right from the start. You know, *To thine own self be true.* It's one of the few things in life over which you have total control."

Spoken like a man who'd given it a lot of thought. Was that because of his wife's problems? she wondered. "Like you always wanted to be a small-town doctor when everybody was trying to convince you to become a surgeon?" He'd been brilliant during his surgical rotation and the offers had flooded in, but he'd turned them down. People had ridiculed him for his choice because rural medicine wasn't in vogue. Wasn't lucrative. Wasn't prestigious.

"Being a surgeon, drinking cinnamon tea, it's all the same thing. Directions that weren't right for me."

She liked that in him. Dermott had a strong sense of self. In her own mixed-up life, a little of that might have helped along the way. "Then would you like to come in for a glass of…?" She didn't remember seeing anything else to serve him but she really didn't want him to leave. "Tap water?"

"Actually, I was going to invite you down for a late supper. Max is in bed now, and I was getting ready to fix myself a grilled cheese sandwich. Since you arrived a day early and I didn't stock you with any food, I thought the least I could do would be to slap a piece of cheese between two slices of bread and throw it in the skillet."

"You wouldn't be offended if I brought my cinnamon tea with me?"

He laughed. "It really is nice to see you, Jenna. I'm glad I didn't run you off on your first day here. Heaven knows, except for my son, not much else had gone right lately. But having you here…"

There was that sad look again. It was hard imagining Dermott as a widower with a young son. But that was his reality and, now, hers. So maybe looking for bits and pieces of the Dermott she'd known years ago was a waste of time. Maybe he'd moved too far from that point for any of it to remain. If so, that would be too bad. But the past was the past, and perhaps he was remaining true to himself as he was now, and not what he used to be. In which case, getting to know him again over a grilled cheese sandwich sounded lovely. "I'm glad I'm here, Dermott. Doubts and all, I'm glad I'm here."

"I hope so, JJ. I really hope so."

She liked it when he called her JJ. That *was* the old Dermott.

* * *

"I have to call her right back," Dermott said. "But I need to run downstairs and check her medical chart to see what her medication dose is. I think she may have taken too much, and that's what's causing her symptoms. Five minutes, and I'll be right back. Then we'll have grilled cheese."

"Can I do anything?"

He shook his head. "I've been changing Mrs. Gray's arthritis medications and she's having some gastric upset because of it, and I suspect she's not taking enough of the medication I prescribed to treat the side effect. Off the top of my head I could guess how many pills she's supposed to take, but I'd rather be safe and check. Do you mind looking after Max for a few minutes?"

"Well, I make a pretty good grilled cheese sandwich myself. You go, I'll cook. And, no, I don't mind looking after Max."

"Jenna Lawson, domestic." He was chuckling on his way out the door. "I'd have never guessed."

Making a sandwich wasn't exactly domestic, but Jenna actually found it rather pleasant puttering around Dermott's kitchen, and she was just about ready to put the skillet on the gas flame when she heard a shriek coming from down the hall. "Max!" she gasped, turning off the gas and running as fast as she could to the bedroom where the little boy was tossing in his bed, and crying. "No!" he cried out. "Don't! Please, don't!"

"Max," she said, running straight to the bed. He was in the throes of a nightmare, and his little body was twisting in the bed. His eyes were open, he was reaching out trying to find something, or someone. Instinctively, Jenna dropped to the side of the bed and pulled the boy into her arms. But he fought her at first, pounding her with his fists, trying to get away.

"No, I don't want to!" he screamed, thrashing, hitting. "No...no...no!"

"Max, it's Jenna. Wake up, Max." She gave him a little shake, but he hit her again. "Max, you're safe. It's Jenna, and I'm here with you. You're safe."

"No," he whimpered, the fight suddenly going out of him. He was drenched in sweat, and he'd wet the bed. "I don't want to," he choked out. "I don't want to."

Jenna held him tight, stroked his head. "You're safe," she whispered. "Nothing's going to hurt you. I promise, nothing's going to hurt you." He must have heard, because he settled down, snuggled into her arms.

"Where's the big guy?" he sniffled. "I want the big guy."

"He's downstairs, talking to a patient. He'll be here in a minute."

"I want him right now!" He pushed away from her and, as if having second thoughts, collapsed back in her arms. "I want him," he said, crying now.

"Shh," she said, starting to rock him. "He's coming right back for you, Max. He's not going to leave you. He'll be right back, I promise."

He nodded, but didn't say anything. His body still shuddered though, and he clung to her as hard as he could. "If he doesn't come back, do I have to go to Grandpa's house?"

"He's coming back. And I'm not going to leave you until he does."

"Promise?"

"Promise." Poor child. He was trying to be brave, but she knew what it was like to have nightmares. She'd had them. Only there'd been no one to hold her like this, no one to take care of her when she'd been so scared, and hadn't known of what. More often than not, her father had hit her and told her to shut up.

"Max!" Dermott gasped, running through the door. He stopped short of the bed, breathless, his face drained of all color. "I heard from downstairs."

"And we're just fine," Jenna said. She was still rocking back and forth with Max in her arms, stroking his hair, holding on to him as tightly as he held her. He had quieted down and seemed contented to stay right where he was. She was contented to have him there, too. "He had a bad dream, but it's over now and he's doing better, aren't you, Max?"

Max nodded, but didn't look up at his dad. His head was still tucked against Jenna's chest, and Jenna held him protectively, the way a mother would. To anyone looking on who didn't know, Jenna could have been his mother, the way she comforted him. Dermott saw that. Saw that she had already become a fierce protector of Max.

"Dermott, we're going to need some fresh pajamas and sheets, if you don't mind getting them. And I think Max would like a quick little bath before he settles back in for the night."

Ten minutes later, after Dermott had gotten Max ready for bed again, and Jenna had changed the bedsheets, Max asked, "Can Jenna read me a story before I go back to sleep?"

"What's your favorite one?" she asked, wondering if Dermott would prefer doing this. She gave him a questioning look, but he smiled, and nodded.

"I wouldn't mind hearing a story from Jenna either." Dermott sighed a huge sigh of relief and slumped down into the chair next to Max's bed. Then he handed her a book. "This is our favorite. We especially like the part where the big, red dump truck wins the race." He looked straight into Jenna's eyes and mouthed the words "Thank you", then settled back to listen to the story.

And so she read, while Max snuggled in again, and Dermott sat across from them, looking totally distracted, trying with everything he had to hold it all back.

After Max was asleep once more, and the grilled cheese sandwiches long forgotten, Dermott walked Jenna to the apartment door. "I'm sorry we put you through that. Max doesn't have these nightmares often—they started after his mother died. But they're so hard on him when he does."

"And hard on you."

"And me," he admitted. He held out his hands to show her they were finally steady again. "I'd much rather it be me than him. When this happens I feel so...so damned helpless. I feel like I'm failing him, and I wonder if he thinks the same thing too, since I'm the one who's supposed to protect him and take care of him, and I can't protect him from these damned nightmares."

She took hold of his hands, both of them, in her hands. "Max doesn't blame you. You're the one he counts on, and the one he asked for when he saw that it was me coming to help him. I promise, you're going to get through this, Dermott. I know it's not so easy right now, and you really can't see past all the pain Max is going through, but you have each other and that's where you'll find the strength you'll need."

He shook his head, struggling with the emotion. "What she did to him..." He choked off his last words, sucked in a sharp breath and let it out slowly. "You were good with Max, Jenna. He was comfortable with you, which he isn't with many people. Thank you for being here for him...and me. And I'm sorry about the grilled cheese sandwiches."

She waved him off on that one. "I'm just upstairs, if you need anything else. And, Dermott, that's a serious offer. If you, or Max, need anything, come and get me."

He pulled her into his arms and hugged her. "I'm glad you're here, JJ. Really glad you're here." Then he returned to Max and Jenna returned to her apartment feeling...good. She was glad she was here, too.

CHAPTER THREE

"WELCOME to Dr. Callahan's office!" Jenna opened the door for the older couple to come inside. They'd been standing on the stoop, refusing to enter, for a good two minutes, and it appeared they were arguing about something. So she'd decided to expedite the matter, whatever it was. "Would you like to come in?"

Neither of them made a move. In fact, the woman took a step backwards.

"Do you have an appointment with the doctor this morning?" Jenna asked.

The old man looked away, but the woman nodded. "I have an appointment with the doctor." She scowled over at her husband. "He has an appointment with something else."

Well, this seemed interesting. But wisely she decided not to butt in. Not at this point in their debate, anyway.

"It's like this every time he brings me here," the woman continued. "He thinks I don't know, thinks I can't smell it all over him, but I do, every single time. And the doctor has warned him, but he doesn't listen. Just doesn't listen." The woman shoved past the door, marched right on by Jenna and went straight to the waiting room, while her little white-haired husband stayed there on the stoop, smiling sheepishly and shrugging.

"I have my routine," he explained. "And it's the only time

I indulge myself. She's out of sorts every time I do, but after fifty years of marriage, I deserve my few minutes."

"Would either of you like a cup of coffee?" she offered, wondering if that would help fix the grumpy mood filling the office.

"Coffee? That's all? Nancy always had sweet rolls out with the coffee," the woman snapped. "So did the other nurse who worked here after her. They made it worth a person's while to come down here and waste her time while her husband was out doing other things."

"I'm sure all Dr. Callahan's nurses were very good."

"Nancy was especially good. Lovely woman." She gave Jenna a skeptical head-to-toe appraisal. "Wonderful nurse, who looked like a nurse *should* look, and took particular pains to be good to the patients. The other nurse, I don't remember her name, was adequate."

A reputation for her to live up to. Somehow, Jenna had a hunch that standing next to the operating table for three hours, pulling back on an abdominal incision while the doctor searched every inch of the man's intestines for an undetected bleeding ulcer was far easier than this was going to be. But this was a small-town practice, Dermott had reminded her. One that was set in its ways. Very set, apparently. "I apologize for not knowing where to buy the sweet rolls. If you tell me, I'll be sure to have them next time you come in."

The old woman's face softened a bit toward Jenna, but when she looked over Jenna's shoulder, her scowl for her husband deepened. "He'd rather indulge in his filthy habits than have a good sweet roll," she said, then sat down. "But, dear, if you'd like to go and get those sweet rolls right now, I'll be glad to sit here and wait. I'll even answer the phone for you."

"Now?" That was a surprise, but the little old lady seemed insistent, and willing to wait to get what she thought was her proper due.

"Two blocks down, on the south side of the street. It's called Linnea's Bakery, and they have a particularly good prune Danish."

"Prune Danish," Jenna repeated.

"Or cheese. That's usually good, too. Although I think the prune might be healthier." The scowl for her husband went up again. "Not that *he* cares about health, with all those filthy habits of his."

"Five minutes, Lorraine. That's all I allow myself. Five lousy minutes, once a week!"

Lorraine... Jenna scanned the appointment book, but didn't find the name there. "I don't see that the doctor has you scheduled for an appointment," she said.

She gave Jenna a look akin to the one she was giving her husband. "Of course he doesn't. I stop in for one of his quick checks every Monday morning—he doesn't charge me anything." Naturally, Lorraine emphasized that last part simply to let Jenna know what was what.

A free physical, a prune Danish, *and* a reputation to live up to? It was time to go and ask Dermott about this. Jenna excused herself and hurried back to Dermott's office as Lorraine was about to start round two with her poor husband.

"Is that Mrs. Ketterman?" Dermott asked, fighting back a mischievous smile. Although his eyes couldn't hide the smile.

"You mean prune Danish?"

He chuckled. "She likes a good cheese Danish too, if Linnea's is out of prune."

"Then she was telling me the truth? That we cater breakfast with our morning appointments?"

"The truth is that Bill Ketterman has a passion for a good cigar, and Lorriane won't allow him to have it at home. So every Monday morning he brings her down for me to check her blood pressure—which is legitimately high—and while she's indulging in Danish, he's indulging himself in the alley."

"And they squabble about it every week like they're doing right now?"

"Sometimes it's worse. I thought they sounded like they were getting along fairly well this morning."

"A marriage made in heaven?"

"A marriage that has endured fifty years. Heaven or hell, that makes it pretty good."

"Fifty years, one man…" She wondered what Dermott would look like in fifty years. Handsome, she decided. The kind of handsome that got better with the years. "So I need to run down to Linnea's, don't I?"

"If Bill is to have his few minutes of pleasure, yes. If you don't mind. I mean, it's not part of your duty, and if you don't want to—"

"Do you indulge all your patients the way you do the Kettermans?" she interrupted.

"They're nice people, and a prune Danish isn't such a big deal. If it makes them feel special in some way, why not? Heaven knows, there are so many things in medicine we can't control, so if a prune Danish makes someone feel better or special or important…" He shrugged. "It's an inexpensive cure for something, I suppose."

This is what made Dermott better than other doctors. He genuinely cared. His compassion was something she'd never forgotten about him. "Anything else I need to know about the patients? And, by the way, I noticed you don't have any appointments scheduled this morning."

"I usually leave the mornings open for anybody who wants to wander in. Then schedule regular appointments in the afternoon, although most people prefer coming in the morning."

"Let me guess. So they can get the prune Danish?"

He nodded. "They'll know what to give you down at Linnea's. Oh, and do you happen to have any kind of a uniform with you?"

She glanced down at her jeans and T-shirt, the outfit Lorraine Ketterman had disapproved of. It wasn't exactly a crisp, professional look…she'd give Lorraine that much. But she didn't have a uniform. "Never wore them. I had some hospital-owned scrubs and they didn't come with me when I left."

"Then grab a white coat out of my office. That'll work, I think. Personally, I don't mind the casual appearance since casual is the way I run the office, but the people here expect to see something more professional…the old-fashioned white uniform, actually."

Sweet rolls and white uniforms. Definitely in keeping with Nancy, the other nurse. He didn't have to say it, but that's what it was. Nancy had set a standard the people here expected, and it was going to be up to Jenna to fit into it. Or distinguish herself in other ways. Like change the bakery order. Skip the Danishes and buy doughnuts. And buy some of those bright floral scrubs of all colors like most nurses wore these days.

Good idea, she decided as she passed by the alley outside, and caught a glimpse of Bill Ketterman standing almost hidden behind the dumpster, a plume of bluish smoke circling his head like a tarnished halo. "Appreciate the sweet rolls, ma'am," he said. "I know they don't seem like much to you, but when you get used to having something…" He paused, sucked in then blew out a puff of smoke. "You like to count on the traditions."

Traditions, like the tray of Danishes she brought back fifteen minutes later. OK, so she'd caved in a little and bought *all* Danishes. But apple and pineapple. For which Mrs. Ketterman was appreciative, especially when she discovered that pineapple was her new favorite flavor.

By the time Lorraine had devoured two of them and received her blood-pressure check, which was normal, three other people had wandered in, none of whom had particularly major complaints. In fact, two of them insisted on not disturbing the doctor, and asked Jenna to take a look. A little sinus congestion, no infection. A little poison ivy, spreading.

A very sparse morning led into what promised to be an even sparser afternoon as there was only one patient scheduled. Someone else who insisted on leaving Dermott alone. Well, it was odd, but for the office nurse it was fulfilling, being the one they wanted to see. And it was nice that Dermott had confidence in her being the first line of medical care, so to speak. But that did leave her wondering, because the people all seemed so sincere about not wanting to disturb him. Could a whole town really be that concerned over the welfare of one of its own?

For someone who hadn't even had a father who'd cared, it was hard to imagine. But she was a little cynical by nature, and she admitted it. A healthy dose of cynicism was an awfully good barrier.

"Big guy!" Max screamed as he ran down the front walk leading away from the Allen house and launched himself into Dermott's open arms.

Dermott scooped up his son and gave him a great big hug. "What have you been doing with yourself all morning? Something blue?"

"Painting that old bed for Jenna! I wanted to paint it red and green, but Grandma said it would look better if it was blue. But Grandpa let me choose which color blue." He grinned from ear to ear.

"Well, the blue on your shirt looks like a very nice blue. Is that the one you chose?"

Max nodded. "Grandma says Jenna will like it if she's smart. Is she smart, big guy?"

"Yes, she's very smart."

"Good, because I heard Grandpa telling Grandma that it wasn't going to be easy. What's not easy? Painting her bed blue?"

Dermott swallowed hard. "What Grandpa said…" He glanced over at his father-in-law, who'd heard Max and was now turning all shades of red.

"Yes, Max. A blue bed isn't so easy to paint, which is why I needed your help," Frank Allen said.

Dermott's heart went out to the man. For all the things Nancy had been, and all the things she'd done, she'd still been Frank's daughter, someone Frank had loved as much as *he* loved Max. "You OK with the arrangements, Frank?" Dermott asked the older man. "Having her live with us was the only way I could afford her."

"OK enough. But to be honest, it's hard seeing another woman taking Nancy's place everywhere. I understand that the two of you were separated and would have probably gone through with the divorce, and don't get me wrong here, I know you need to move on, and we want you to, but…"

Frank was entitled to his feelings, but Dermott was entitled to his own, and part of those feelings were about concealing all the ugly truths from Nancy's family. Sure, they knew she'd abused drugs. Everyone in town had found that out at the time of Nancy's accident, and he'd spent the months since then trying to hide everything else. Especially from Nancy's parents. Would it do them any good to know that when she'd been high she had also abused Max? That she'd had other men in her life? That she'd stolen her drugs from his own medical supplies?

The answer was no. They didn't need any more pain. "She's not taking over, Frank. Just stepping in and helping me where I need it," Dermott said, lowering Max to the ground. "I know the people here are determined to slow down their medical care so I can have more time with Max, and I appreciate that, but I need help even with the way I've cut back, and I am thinking about growing the practice back up again because I do miss my work. So I need an office nurse who might be able to bring back a few of my straying patients." The people here deserved the convenience of more medical care at home and he did want to give that. It was part of making his life normal once more, but it was also his duty.

"My daughter—she was a good nurse, though, wasn't she, Dermott?" Frank asked.

"You know how much the people here loved her, loved the way she went out of her way to do the nice things for them. They still talk about her with affection, Frank. Even Lorraine Ketterman, and you know how grumpy she can get." Sure, it was a generic thing to say, but it was the truth. Noncommittal, but true. And it's what Frank needed to hold on to—the side of his daughter that people had adored. He was holding hard, because he was smiling now. But Dermott saw pain behind that smile—the pain Frank never talked about.

Dermott gave his father-in-law an affectionate squeeze on the shoulder. "So, are you two men going to finish up that blue bed this afternoon?"

Max looked up at his dad, grinned, gave him a big, blue, double thumbs-up sign. "Can you come and see it, big guy?" Max asked, then took off running down the path to the barn.

Dermott and Frank followed at a slower pace. "I don't mean to overstep the mark, Dermott. Under the circumstances, it's generous of you letting us have Max with us so much. He makes up for, well…you know."

"Not generous, Frank. I need you to look after him. You're the only ones I trust to do that." So very true. He was a lucky man, having them in his life the way he did, and no matter what it took, he intended on keeping them there. "Besides, Max loves coming here. It's good for him. Gives him something to do other than hang around an old building all day."

At the barn, Dermott got a good look at Max's work of art. "You're right, Max," Dermott said, biting back a laugh. "It is a good color. Did Grandpa give you permission to paint all the wooden columns in his barn with those blue happy faces, by the way?" Dermott sighed a contented sigh. Happy faces, happy life. Too bad it couldn't be that way all the time.

* * *

"You're the new nurse," the woman behind the lunch counter said on her way around to show Jenna to a table by the front window. "I heard you did a good job on Isaiah Wilkerson last night."

The woman, whose name tag read Sadie, seemed pleasant. She was about Jenna's age. Platinum-blonde hair. A figure even the most well endowed would envy. Voluptuous didn't begin to go far enough in describing her. And she had a friendly smile, too. That's what Jenna liked, the smile. It was like the one so many of the people here turned on her and, to be honest, the genuine warmth in Fort Dyott felt good all the way down to the bone. It was a place she *could* call home, she thought. "Did you hear that from Isaiah?" she asked.

"Him, and about thirteen other people. Isaiah said you were very kind to him, and I'm guessing that wasn't easy. He's a stubborn man. And I can say that because he's my uncle."

"He was a little stubborn, come to think of it." Jenna's eyes twinkled with laughter. This was a nice place, she felt welcome here. "But I've had worse. All things considered, he wasn't even on my list of the ten worst patients I've ever had."

Sadie returned Jenna's laughter. "Worse? Tell that to my aunt. She had a fit last night when she found out what had happened and he hadn't even called her. And she had a bigger fit when she found out he'd actually thought about driving himself all the way over to Muledeer."

"Because he didn't want to disturb the doctor."

"Doc Callahan's had a rough few months and we're just trying to help out. There's so little you can really do when someone…well, dies, you know? And time is such an easy thing to give him, especially now, when he needs it with his son."

"Except you've got to balance common sense with that."

"Tell that to Uncle Isaiah. He still thinks he should have gone to Muledeer. He was Nancy's schoolteacher for a couple of years, so he wants to be supportive to her family right now."

"Nancy?"

"Nancy Allen. Dr. Callahan's wife, and office nurse."

"Her name was Nancy?" Interesting, how Dermott had never mentioned her name. More interesting that the legendary nurse Nancy had also been Dermott's wife.

Sadie nodded yes. "Frank and Irene Allen's daughter. It was so sad, how it happened."

Something was telling Jenna that Nancy hadn't died from a drug overdose, as she'd assumed. But Sadie wasn't the one to ask about that. "So tell me, what's good today?"

"Chicken salad. That's the special. It has raisins in it." Sadie gave her nod of approval, so that's what Jenna ordered, along with an iced tea. Then she enjoyed a leisurely lunch where at least a dozen people stopped by her table, thanking her for coming to work in Fort Dyott, for helping Dermott. Then she returned to her apartment to spend the remainder of her two-hour break unpacking the rest of her clothes and settling in for good. And wondering about Nancy.

Finally down to her last clothes to put away—her undies— Jenna stared at them for a moment, realizing how symbolic putting them away would be. Cold feet set in. Her natural reaction. She wanted to put them away, was afraid to. Needed to.

"Damn," she muttered, throwing them on the floor. "Damn, damn, damn!" One little thing. One simple little thing, and she couldn't do it. Couldn't make that kind of a commitment. *Pick them up, Jenna. Put them away, Jenna.* That's all she had to do. *Come over here and take your punishment before Daddy has to get more angry with you than he already is, Jenna. Daddy really doesn't want to hurt you again, but you make him do it. You're such a bad, bad girl.*

"You OK?" Dermott called from the hall. "I heard you shouting."

No, she wasn't OK. Not with a lot of things. "I'm fine," she said, stepping over her undies on the way to the door. Beads of nervous perspiration dotted her face. Her hands shook. Her stomach knotted. "Just fine."

"I trust you had a nice lunch?" Dermott asked. Shrugging into his white coat, he glanced out the front window and stared at the bustling little road for a moment. It did lead away from Fort Dyott, and he'd thought about that from time to time. Thought about loading Max into the car and simply driving until he found another place that looked like home to him. There was a doctor shortage in the area, he could find a job anywhere. But Max needed to be here to be near his grandparents. He'd already had so much disruption in his young life, and Dermott wasn't about to cause more. So every time he thought about taking to the road, he turned his thoughts to the only thing he and Nancy had done right. For a man who'd never given a whole lot of thought to being a father, it was all he thought about nowadays. All he wanted to be. "Sorry I ran off and left you, but Max and I have a standing peanut butter and jelly lunch together every day, unless there's an emergency."

"Grape jelly?" Jenna asked.

"Is there any other kind?"

"Sometimes strawberry is good."

Dermott shook his head. "On toast, but never on peanut butter. That's serious stuff."

"Where is he when you're working?"

"With his grandparents. They're great with Max. Love him to pieces, spoil him rotten. I don't know what I'd do without them."

"Then you're lucky. My dad was a single father, and he left me alone a good bit of the time. Eventually I went to live with my grandparents, and it was better. So I know how nice it is to have them around to help you with Max. Nice for both of you."

"Your grandparents raised you?" Honestly, he really didn't know much about Jenna's background. She'd never spoken of it and on the couple of times he'd asked questions, she hadn't answered. What he remembered was…evasion?

"For a while."

Dermott turned away from the window. "No mother?"

"She lived a hard life, and died young. I think she simply gave up when she couldn't face it any longer. At least, to a little girl, that's what it seemed like."

"I'm sorry, JJ. I do know how rough that is. So your father…"

"Was a busy man," she said, her voice thin and tight.

"Which is why you went to your grandparents' home?" She wasn't comfortable with this. Not at all, and this was a side of Jenna he'd never seen before. She was blank. Totally blank. No emotion, no expression. Nothing, except answers by rote from a woman who was always exuberant with her opinions. It made him wonder why, but he wouldn't ask. A man who had his own secrets to hide had no business asking someone about theirs.

"It's every child's dream to live on a ranch, isn't it? And I was lucky enough to have that dream come true for a while."

Oh, so hurt. And defensive. It was written all over her. So much so he wanted to pull her into his arms and make it better. He wouldn't, of course. But that didn't stop the longing in him to do so. Time to get off the subject, though, because the closer he got to her problems, the closer he got to his own, and, heaven only knew, that was the last thing he wanted to do. It was time to quit trying to be involved personally or romantically, to quit thinking he actually could get involved again. "Max wants a horse, but he's too young."

"That's what he told me. He has all kinds of plans for riding lessons, the kind of saddle he wants to buy, the name he'll give his own horse when you buy him one."

"He's been talking to you?"

"Some. You know, the usual things. Will the big guy buy him a gray horse or a black one?"

Max was more of an observer these days and, except for family, he really didn't talk much to other people. So with the way he'd clung to her during his nightmare, and now this, Dermott was encouraged. His son felt safe with her, and there'd been a time when Dermott wasn't sure that Max would ever feel truly safe with *any* woman other than his grandmother. So this was good. "Look, JJ. I'm sorry I've been so preoccupied since you got here, and all you seem to do is get hit with problems."

"You have been preoccupied, haven't you?" she agreed, a look of relief washing over her face for the new direction in their conversation. "And maybe a little ill mannered. Oh, and a bad host," she teased.

"Ill mannered?" He recalled other banter between them years ago. Damned sexy. And fun. "Bad host? That's just your opinion."

"My opinion, yes. And it's correct, of course."

She kept a perfectly straight face, but had to bite her lip to keep from smiling. He could see that. It reminded him of the first time he'd kissed her. They'd been going back and forth over which syringe needle gauge to use when giving an injection to a patient. He'd liked a bigger needle for its ease of medicine delivery. She'd liked using a smaller one, for patient comfort. Twenty-gauge, thirty gauge. They'd gone on and on about it for minutes, light, nearly flirtatious banter, ending with Jenna volunteering to give him an injection with each size needle to see which he'd prefer. "Drop your pants, Doctor, and I'll stick you in the bottom with one of each to see which feels better to you."

"Only if I can do the same to you," he'd said. "Turnabout's fair, you know."

"Then you go first," she retorted.

"I think you just want to see my bum," he'd come right back at her.

She'd looked him square in the eye, practically no smile on her face, just like now, and said, "A beautiful bum is a beautiful bum, Doctor. What I'd prefer is seeing the expression on your face when I stick you in your beautiful bum with a twenty-gauge."

He'd nearly lost his heart to her that day. He did lose the argument, without dropping his pants. On the bright side, though, he'd stolen a kiss, which had turned out to be the best victory of all. Just a quick one, as her stern facade had finally crumpled into a smile and she'd started laughing. Then he'd started laughing, and...well, he remembered the kiss. Remembered wondering if that would happen again.

As it turned out, he hadn't had to wait too long for the next one. Good days, he thought.

Now, well...he knew it wouldn't happen, but couldn't help thinking about it. And he did enjoy the banter between them. It was nice, being reminded of old times. "Like I admitted, I'm a little preoccupied. I'll even concede the ill-mannered part. Grudgingly. But bad host?" He shook his head. "A beautiful host is a beautiful host, Nurse."

She looked properly surprised for a moment, then surprise melted into a full, sunshiny smile. "You remember that day?"

"Our first kiss? How could I forget it?" *Dangerous, dangerous stuff*, Dermott, he warned himself. *You're playing with fire.* Fire that would eventually burn him if he wasn't careful, because natural urges didn't vanish simply because he wanted them to. He was going to have to go about this relationship very, very carefully because he had Max to think about now. Between his son and his medical practice, there wasn't enough of him left over for anything or anyone else.

"Well, it wasn't exactly the most romantic situation, was it?" She smiled, remembering.

"And we weren't exactly the most romantic couple."

Jenna's eyes fairly sparkled. "I don't remember that we were actually an official couple. More like two people skating around the edges of involvement, but not really ever entering the circle."

"Well, it wasn't for a lack of trying, because you could have had me in that circle any time you wanted, Jenna. You knew that. Then that day we got caught in the closet…" There had never been anybody in his life since who'd affected him the way Jenna had. Yes, they'd already slept together by that day. Frantically. Wildly. So many times in such a few weeks, and it had never been enough. Once, or twice, or a million times with Jenna was never enough. Then that day in the hospital, they'd teased each other, exchanged suggestive whispers in the hall, sent looks that had left nothing to the imagination. In any other place they'd have been out of their clothes and onto better things in the blink of an eye. That's just the way they'd been. But that day, in the hospital…he'd wanted her in every way a man could want a woman and she'd wanted him just as badly. The closet had been out of the way, convenient, they had both been on a break…and forgotten to lock the door.

Well, he'd served out the last weeks of his residency with a few pats on the back from admirers, a few suggestive winks, a few bawdy if not jealous comments from colleagues. Jenna…she'd transferred to another department the next day and taken a job at another hospital the next week.

That had been the end of that. He'd called her, gone to her apartment, banged on her door, left notes, sent flowers. But she'd moved away. No notice. No forwarding address.

Sure, he could have found her. He knew where she worked for a while after that, until she changed jobs again. But what was the point? She'd made herself clear. It was over. They were finished.

"Different times, different people," she said on a wistful sigh. "Young and foolish, young and hormonal, take your pick." Then she sobered up. "Why didn't you tell me that Nancy your nurse was also Nancy your wife?"

"Didn't I?"

"No."

"Oversight, I guess."

"Was it really?"

Maybe it wasn't. Maybe he didn't want Jenna to think that his judgment was so depleted that he could have invested so much in a woman who'd done bad things to him both professionally and personally. It was one thing to say that he hadn't noticed what his wife was doing, and that was true for quite a while. But to admit that he didn't know his office nurse was stealing drugs? It made him look like a fool, being so blind to everything, trusting someone who'd falsified the office pharmaceutical records. So maybe what he was doing was trying to save face in Jenna's eyes, because what she thought of him mattered.

Well, so much for that! And so much for the pleasant few moments they'd just spent.

Without saying another word, Dermott spun around and marched into his office, his footsteps thudding heavily against the wooden ground. When he got there, he slammed the door so hard it knocked his medical diploma off the wall. He looked at it lying on the floor for a moment before he bent to pick it up, studying the writing on it, thinking about all it stood for. Dermott Maxwell Callahan, Doctor of Medicine. Graduated with honors, top of his class.

He was a doctor, sworn to serve, to help, to heal. And he was a miserable failure right here in his office, where all that mattered most. Damn, where had he gone so wrong?

The fit of anger and frustration in him boiled over so hard that after he picked it up Dermott threw the diploma at the wall, shattering its glass as it hit, and knocking over a pottery lamp on its way to the floor. That too fell, and broke.

"Dermott?" Jenna called from outside in the hall. "Are you OK?"

He didn't answer. Should have, but he wasn't OK. Nothing was OK.

"Dermott. Just say something, will you?"

Damn, he hated himself.

"Dermott, please…"

"I don't talk about her," he finally yelled. "OK? I just don't talk about her." Balling his fists, he wanted to punch the wall, but he didn't. That would only injure his hand, then Jenna would have to fix him up which would lead to…more talk. But he was talked out on the subject. Emotionally drained. Tired. So, rather than doing something stupid, he slipped into his chair and turned to look out the window at the road, wondering, once again, what it would be like to take it. Just pack up his son and go somewhere where no one knew him.

CHAPTER FOUR

"It's a lovely blue!" Jenna exclaimed, as Frank adjusted the bed rails. "How did you know that blue was my favorite color?"

Max beamed. "I guessed. But I almost thought it was purple."

"Well, since purple is my second favorite color, I would have loved having a purple bed, too."

"And I'd have had a purple barn," Frank said, laughing. He scooted the bedframe back into the corner of the room then stood back to appraise his handiwork. "Well, that should do it. I'll have Dermott help me carry the mattress up and you'll have a proper bed tonight instead of that old rollaway you've been using."

"I haven't seen him yet today," Jenna said. She hadn't seen him last night, either. In fact, it had been a long, lonely night all by herself. She'd gone back to the diner for dinner, taken a walk then retired to…well, nothing. To be honest, she wasn't used to such a lack of activity or stimulation, and that nursing journal she'd buried herself in, while informative, wasn't stimulating. "He hasn't come into the office." And hadn't told her why, but she had an idea it had something to do with the residual effects of last night. She'd hit a very raw nerve, and she did feel bad about that because Dermott seemed to be juggling so many things, including a fair share of guilt. She really didn't want to make it worse for him.

"He's having a rough time of it now," Frank said, then immediately glanced at Max, who'd climbed into the middle of the empty bedframe and was getting ready to roll one of his toy cars from one end to the other. Bending to pick up his tools, Frank huffed out an impatient sigh, but didn't finish what he was saying.

"We used to be friends," she said, not sure why she felt compelled to. "Years ago."

"He mentioned that. Said you were a competent nurse, which is why he wanted you here." He stood up and gave her a long, thoughtful appraisal. "Dermott's life is his own business, Miss Lawson. I don't interfere, I don't express opinions. But let me tell you this much. He's a good man. Most people wouldn't let us have the involvement Dermott lets us have with Max, and my wife and I owe him a lot for what he's done to keep the boy in our lives. But Dermott is dealing with a difficult situation, and he doesn't need any more pressure than he's already got on him."

"You think I'd do that? Cause him more pressure?"

"Maybe not intentionally. But things aren't normal for him, the way they used to be before my daughter…" He paused, swallowed hard. "All I'm saying is, whatever it is you're expecting to find here may not be what's really here. See it for what it is, Miss Lawson. Not for what you want it to be and it'll work out for both of you—however you want it to work out."

She wasn't sure what that meant. Was it a warning for her to keep away from Dermott, or a blessing to get involved with him? "What I want is a job I love. That's why I came here."

"Is it?"

That was a question she couldn't answer because, the truth be told, she probably wouldn't have accepted the position, such as it was, from a stranger. Which meant Dermott's father-in-law was one very perceptive man. "I love being a nurse, and that's always my first priority. I'm not trying to step in and take your daughter's place, if that's what you think I'm doing."

"Except that you're doing her job, living in her building, having a relationship with her husband *and* her son."

"*Professional* relationship." Jenna glanced over at Max, who was so caught up in racing his little cars that he didn't even know anybody else was in the room with him. Or did he? He was a perceptive little boy. An observer, Dermott had called him. So, how much had he observed when no one was noticing, when the adults around him underestimated how much a young child was taking in? *Like Frank was doing right now.* "Dermott and I had a good working relationship years ago, and that's what I'm trying to re-establish right now. *All* I'm trying to re-establish." She felt sorry for Frank. It had to be so difficult seeing another woman in all the places he was used to seeing his daughter. "I appreciate you setting up the bed," she said. Then to Max, "And you couldn't have picked a better color. In fact, it's the best blue bed I've ever seen."

"I'm going to ask the big guy if I can paint my bed blue, too. Maybe blue *and* purple! Can I use your paint, Grandpa?"

Frank chuckled. "I think that's a project I'll let your dad help you with."

The phone downstairs rang just as the bell over the door jingled, and Jenna dashed down the stairs ahead of Frank and Max, pulling on Dermott's oversized white coat as she did so. Waving at the young woman standing in the waiting room, she got to the phone on the fourth ring. It was a woman named Barbara who wanted to know if Jenna could have a look at her daughter. The child had a sore throat, no fever, and Barbara thought that since it didn't seem serious maybe Jenna could do the exam. Not a good situation, but Jenna asked Barbara to bring her daughter in. Then she turned her attention to the young woman in the waiting room. "May I help you?"

"My grandmother…" She hesitated, like she wasn't sure if this was such a good idea.

"Does she need to see a doctor?" Jenna prompted.

The woman first nodded, then shook her head. "I'm not

sure what she needs. She's been down for a few days now, and she doesn't have the energy to get up and do much. She's losing weight, too, but I'm not sure she's really sick. She says she feels well enough, but..."

"These are recent changes?"

"Yes. Until a few days ago, she walked a couple of kilometers a day, still rode her bicycle a few times a week. Then she took to her bed and she won't let me call a doctor. *Refuses* to let me call one, actually. So you can see what kind of problem I'm having. On top of that, I can't stay here much longer. My husband and children need me at home. So, I thought that since you're not a doctor... I mean, I know it's sneaky, but I don't know what else I can do."

"Will she be needing a house call, or do you think she could make it into the office?"

"At home, I think. She's staying close to the bed."

In the end, Jenna promised to drop in on Leona Hazelwood after she'd had a look at Barbara Moorehouse's daughter, Emily, whom she was seeing immediately after she assisted Dermott with their ten o'clock appointment with Tom Parker's mysterious rash.

"I understand that the famous blue bed has arrived," Dermott said from his office a while later, as Jenna busied herself for the first appointment of the day.

"And a nice blue bed it is." He was sitting at his desk, looking rather fetching in his white coat. Smiling, but the smile was strained, a little unsure. It was an attempt, though, and she appreciated it.

"I heard rumors that there might be a blue bed in *my* future."

"That's between the painter of the blue bed and his father."

"I'm sorry about yesterday, Jenna. Sorry that I wasn't honest with you about Nancy, too. It's easier *not* talking about her, and sometimes I feel cornered when I have to."

Living life a few steps away from the reality of it. Well, if anybody understood how it felt to be cornered by reality, she did. But she didn't have anybody so connected to her that *her* avoidance of anything made a difference. Dermott did, and in some way, deep down, it had to make a real difference knowing that the avoidances had a purpose. "You know, I really don't want to get into the middle of this. With what I've been through I don't need another person's problems, but, like it or not, I'm getting dragged in and you're not being helpful about it. And I don't even get the impression that you care what's going on."

"I care," he said, his voice as brittle as ice. "That's the problem. Because if I didn't care I'd get the hell out of here so fast…" Dermott paused for a moment, shut his eyes and drew in a long, deep breath. When he'd exhaled it, he opened his eyes again. "My marriage was hell, Jenna. In so many ways. I jumped in too soon, didn't know her well enough. Probably had residual feelings left over for someone else."

Her? Thinking that she might have been the one he'd had feelings for caused her pulse to quicken a little.

"And when things started changing, there was no one to turn to. I was married to the town's fair-haired child who was changing more and more every day. She needed drugs to wake her up in the morning, drugs to help her sleep, drugs to make her feel better during the day. Nancy did so many good things, but she had such a dark side to her that I simply couldn't deal with because no one believed it was there." He shrugged. "Sometimes the obvious isn't easy to see, especially when you don't want to, and nobody wanted to. Including me."

"I'm so sorry, Dermott. I had no idea how bad it was. When you said she had a drug dependence…"

"That's a nice way to put it, JJ. She was addicted. It changed her personality. Pitted people against each other, which she enjoyed doing. Like she enjoyed hiding it until the point when she couldn't any longer."

"Some drug addicts are very good at hiding it." Like some alcoholics. Like her father.

"You'd think a doctor would notice, though, wouldn't you? Or a husband?"

"Except you weren't seeing her as a doctor. And I expect that when your marriage started going bad, you weren't seeing *anything* very clearly." At least now she understood why he was spending so much time with Max. Dermott felt guilty for spending so little time with his wife and he blamed himself for what had happened to her. "She was an educated woman, Dermott. A nurse. She knew what she was doing when she took those drugs...knew better than most people."

"But was she trying to get my attention? Is that why she was doing it? Or was that always in her and I simply didn't know it when we married?"

"Don't make it that personal. With addiction, it's not about the other person. It's about what the addict wants. They may lay the blame somewhere else, because that's the easiest way to justify what they're doing, but if you're the one having the blame thrown at you, you have to fight your way through the guilt to realize that another person's addiction is their choice, not your fault." And so sad for everyone involved.

"You sound like someone who has some experience."

She hadn't meant to do this, but she had to. After so many years, there were no more avoidances for this, because Dermott needed to hear it. He needed her honesty. "I do. My father was an alcoholic. There was never a day he was sober, and I did get help through a program when I went to live with my grandparents." Until she'd quit and run away.

"Then you know why I have to protect Max the way I do. What his mother did, he doesn't need that brought down on him again. He needs someone to keep it all away from him."

"Have you ever thought that you over-protect him?"

"Maybe I do."

She smiled. "Of course you do. That's who you are." The

old Dermott. She was glad he was still there. Damaged and discouraged, but there in all the ways that mattered.

His eyes went soft for a moment, soft and distant, and she could see the pain. It was profound and raw. At that moment she could feel his pain as surely as if it were hers. She didn't understand it fully yet, but she knew its depths, knew how hard it was for him to talk about it. As hard as it was for her to talk about her pain, and her father's addiction. No, she hadn't told him everything. But it was a start and, surprisingly, she didn't feel too bad for it. Maybe because it was for Dermott's sake. And for Max. Or maybe because Dermott simply made things easier for her.

"So, we've got a rash to deal with," she said, deliberately changing the subject. A little emotion spent went a long way, and she was emotionally exhausted. The look on Dermott's eyes told her he was, too.

He sighed, visibly grateful to be back to the topic of medicine. "Ah, yes. Contact dermatitis. Weed poisoning. He doesn't like to wear socks and yet he likes to walk out in the wilds. Gets him every time, right around the ankles. Red rash, tiny pinprick-sized bumps, itchy, dry. He scratches, it gets worse, until he needs a shot of cortisone and some pills for follow-up."

"Impressive. You know your patients well. So tell me about Leona Hazelwood. She's my house call who refuses to see a doctor."

"She refuses because the doctor knows she's not ill. It's loneliness. Physically, she'll be fine. Heartier than most seventy-year-olds. But her family gets busy, they forget to call for a while, don't make that two-hour drive in to see her as often as they should, and she gets sick. Classic symptoms— she's weak, just doesn't feel well, loses a pound or two because she refuses to eat, even though she has a stash of chocolate hidden in her bedroom. It brings one of her daughters or granddaughters running and two or three days later Leona has a miracle cure. She's up and back to normal."

Jenna laughed. "No wonder she refuses to see you. So what do you advise I do for her?"

"Give her a good check-up. At her age, it doesn't hurt. Then a nice little shot of vitamin B12. I'll prescribe it, you'll give it."

Jenna laughed. "B12? It's just a vitamin, doesn't cure anything."

"On the contrary, it cures a plethora of ills. Just not any medical ones." He smiled. "She'll be up and out of bed by this evening, eating a fairly normal meal again, and tomorrow morning she'll feel like taking a short walk. After her granddaughter leaves town, she'll be happy for weeks."

"Does Leona know she's faking?"

"Probably. Although I haven't told her so. Why spoil a good round of sympathy and attention with something so unnecessary? But she's smart, and while I don't think she exactly plans her sick spells, I'm pretty sure she's onto them, which is why she doesn't want a doctor taking a look and calling her a hypochondriac. I like to think of it as being manipulative in a sweet little granny way."

"And if a sweet little granny can't be manipulative, who can?"

"You go take care of the granny, I'll take care of the rash, and maybe we can have lunch together afterwards? We've got a new jar of grape jelly."

"Could we stop at the grocery for some strawberry?"

He smiled. "I'm not the boss of the peanut butter sandwiches, but Max likes you. He thinks you have very good taste in blue beds, so I suppose strawberry will be fine."

"Blue and purple," Jenna corrected.

"Is there something going on I don't know about?"

She laughed. "I think this should be one of those special father-and-son moments." Then she scampered down the hall, drew up a syringe of B12, grabbed her medical bag and waved a greeting to Tom Parker, who was hunched over, scratching his ankles, as she hurried to the door. At the door, she paused for a moment, went back to Tom Parker, whispered something in his ear, then dashed out the door.

"She took her shot?" Dermott asked, as he slathered the strawberry on the peanut butter. Peanut butter sandwich, glass of cold milk.

"Like a trouper. And it's amazing how quick that B12 took hold. Her granddaughter agreed to stay the night and leave tomorrow rather than this afternoon."

"Why's that?"

"I asked her to keep an eye on Leona for a reaction to the shot. Just one night. I figured that would give Leona a little bonus time she probably wasn't counting on. Oh, and I talked to Leona about buying a computer, so she can have access to e-mail. She claims she's too old, but I promised that I'd show her how to use it if she decided to get it, and that way she could have almost instant access to all her family, anytime. I explained that the problem with the phone nowadays is that people don't always have time to talk when someone calls, but an e-mail can be answered at a person's leisure, and that she could actually write one e-mail and send it out to everyone at the same time, if she wanted. And I mentioned that she could have a camera in it to get live pictures."

"You're devious." Dermott placed the sandwiches on plates and pointed to the pitcher of milk. "You carry that and the glasses, and I think we're set for lunch."

"Not devious. Just trying to think of ways to help Leona feel better. Her granddaughter said she was going to ask the whole family to pitch in on the cost of the computer." She followed Dermott out the door, to the picnic table in the back yard. "Do Frank and Irene join you?"

"Not usually. Most of the time it's just Max and me. They know we like our time together, and I think after a morning of

Max and his high-volume energy, they're glad to have a little rest."

"Am I'm butting in? Are you sure Max won't mind because I could go to the diner."

"And leave me stuck with strawberry jam on peanut butter? Who'd eat it?"

"But I don't want to interrupt your time with Max."

Like the rest of town, but Jenna could never, ever be an interruption. "Trust me, you're not interrupting. And Max won't mind. If I thought he would, I wouldn't have suggested it."

"You're a good father," she said, sitting down at the table.

"A good enough father with a pretty damned good kid."

"Not just good enough, Dermott. Any father who'd eat peanut butter sandwiches every day with his kid is a very good father. Especially when that father doesn't like peanut butter."

He looked over at her. "What makes you think I don't like peanut butter?"

"You told me. We took a break together once, and went down to the staff lounge to grab a sandwich from the vending machine. You accidentally punched the button for a peanut butter and jelly, and you threw it in the trash when you got it because you said you hated peanut butter. You got a ham and cheese instead."

"You remembered that?" It had happened, and he hadn't thought of it until now. So why had she remembered something so insignificant about him? Maybe for the same reason *he'd* remembered so many insignificant things about her.

Jenna shrugged. "Of course I remembered it. I had to loan you enough money to buy that other sandwich."

He hoped she'd remembered for some other reason than that, and he was a little disappointed. But Jenna did sidestep her feelings, didn't she? So she could have remembered because... Well, he wouldn't finish that thought. But what she claimed wasn't necessarily the real reason. And on that thought, he relaxed a little. "Did I ever pay you back?"

"I don't think so."

"Then I owe you, don't I?"

She held up her peanut butter and strawberry jam sandwich. "I think you've just paid me back. So tell me, why do you eat something you don't like? Couldn't you and Max have ham and cheese sandwiches instead? Or alternate between ham and cheese, and peanut butter and jelly?"

"We could, but this is his favorite and he likes the idea that it's my favorite, too. So what's one sandwich in the course of a day?" He studied Jenna for a moment, as she cut her halved sandwich into quarters. There was so much there, so many layers to her. Years ago he hadn't looked much past the obvious assets, and while they were stunning in ways that the years had only enhanced, everything else about her was stunning, too. Here he was being almost mean to her, yet she was looking for ways to make it all good. "Wash it down with enough milk and it's not so bad."

She handed him a quarter of her sandwich. "Try it. You might change your mind."

"You're being devious again."

"Practical. Not devious. Connect one lady with her family on a more regular basis and that's even better than a shot of B12. Tell one man that if he doesn't wear socks and continues getting these rashes, then accidentally forgets to wash his hands after scratching it once, he could spread that nasty rash to, well...you know where. Connect that rash to a man's more sensitive parts and I'll bet that man puts on a pair of socks next time he takes to the wilds."

"You told him that? Because he was awfully agreeable for once. And here I thought I was the one who was finally convincing him to mend the error of his sockless ways!" Damn, she was good! And the peanut butter wasn't half bad with the strawberry, either. Or maybe it was Jenna who made it better.

Either way, tomorrow he'd give Max a choice between grape and strawberry. Broaden some narrow male horizons for both of them.

"So, what's this your grandfather is telling me about a new painting project?" Dermott asked Max, who plopped down at the picnic table and immediately dove into his sandwich.

"Going to paint my bed," he said, with his mouth full. When he'd swallowed, he continued, "Jenna and I are going to paint it blue and purple. Then we're going to paint my bedroom walls blue and purple, too."

"You and Jenna?" He glanced over at Jenna, who gave him an innocent shrug. "Whose idea was it?"

"Hers," Max replied in all confidence. "She said she likes blue and purple, and so do I."

"Have you asked her to help you do this?"

He didn't answer because his mouth was full of sandwich again, but he gave his head a vigorous shake.

"Should you ask her to help, since it was her idea?"

At that, Max shrugged, much more interested in finishing his sandwich and getting to the plate of huge, gooey chocolate-chip cookies his grandmother had baked earlier.

"So tell me, Jenna, about your passion for purple and blue," Dermott teased.

"Actually, the passion is for blue and purple, with blue being the predominant color. Of course, Max may disagree with me on that, and decide he'd rather go predominantly purple. His choice, since it's his room."

"And you volunteered to help?"

"Well, not in so many words, but I think I can find some time to fit it into my schedule."

Then it was Max's idea. That was amazing, because Max had withdrawn so much after Nancy's death. With all the abuse he'd suffered from her in those last months, the child psychologist had said it was only natural that Max wouldn't be so outgoing with people. The psychologist had also said it was natural for Max to be so clingy to him and to Nancy's parents. They were the only stability Max recognized and trusted. Now Jenna was included in that, and it pleased him more and more each time he saw it. Other people Max knew much better than he knew Jenna had tried to get through to him these past months—parents of friends, friends he normally played with, other people he'd been raised around—and he wanted nothing to do with any of them. But Jenna...

So what if Max was about to turn his bedroom into a hideous combination of purple and blue, or, as Jenna put it, blue and purple? It was an amazing step in the right direction and a huge sense of relief after so much worry.

For the first time in months Dermott allowed himself to feel the slightest touch of optimism. "So, can you let me in on these plans you and Max made?" he asked, reaching over and taking another quarter of her sandwich, and replacing it with half of his.

"Actually, I think Max is the master architect on this project. You'll have to ask him."

They both looked over at the boy, who was fist deep in his glass of milk, dunking his chocolate-chip cookie. This felt good, the three of them having lunch like this. More than good, it felt normal—a normalcy he wanted to last.

CHAPTER FIVE

PEOPLE trickled in with minor complaints throughout the afternoon. Some specifically requested Jenna, and others insisted that Dermott treat them. It was a sporadic flow, leaving Jenna not quite so discouraged about her future at the clinic. The truth was, when the clinic was in operation, Dermott did need a nurse, which was a good thing because, more and more, a big part of her wanted to stay in Fort Dyott for a while.

"Have you ever thought about updating to a computer?" she asked as he was heading into one exam room while she was on her way to another. "The old-fashioned way of storing charts works, but there are so many good medical practice programs out there, and I think you could save yourself some time and effort by upgrading your methods."

"You don't like my methods?" Dermott asked, giving her a suggestive smile.

"Some of your methods are fine," she said, a shy smile turning up the corners of her mouth, "but some need a little help."

"Then help away. You're free to do whatever you like but keep in mind that at some point you'll have to teach me and I'm technologically challenged. I like my games on an old-fashioned board that you pull down off the closet shelf and dust off, and I like my music on vinyl. That nice, scratchy needle going round and round on a record gives it a sound you'll never get on a CD."

"Not CD any more, Dermott."

"See what I mean?"

Jenna laughed. That explained his outdated office. It was a preference, and while she didn't believe that Dermott was as technologically challenged as he wanted her to believe, she did think that his choices more reflected a simpler lifestyle. And she liked that. In fact, she found great appeal in that because she admired the kind of strength it took to buck the system. In his own way, that's exactly what Dermott did here. He stuck to what he wanted no matter what people said, *no matter what she said*, which made him a man of conviction. "But we are keeping the electricity, aren't we?" she teased.

Chuckling, he said, "It's a good thing, in moderation. But there's also something to be said for getting away from that, too. You know, the nice glow of candlelight."

Immediately, visions of a romantic evening with Dermott waltzed through her thoughts. They were embracing, kissing, then they were… Nothing! They were nothing because that's not what he meant and she knew it. But it was still a pleasant fantasy. Jenna cleared her throat, forcing herself back to the conversation at hand. "Problem is, if you get *too* far away, your cellphone won't work."

"I thought you had more adventure in you than that, JJ."

His eyes crinkled with a smile that practically melted her. And with the supply closet positioned right behind them, the way it was, this was getting dangerous. The fantasies fighting their way back in were even more dangerous. So why was she was so attracted, given all her reservations? Given all her convictions?

It was crazy. Didn't make sense when weighing all the problems they both had. Yet she flirted outrageously with the man. Watched him. Had very sexy fantasies about him. Couldn't help herself. Even something as innocent as an enquiry about updating to a computer system turned into a pretty obvious flirtation. "So, about that computer…" she said, trying to get herself back on track yet again.

"Want to talk more about it over dinner? Max and I are having canned spaghetti tonight. It's not gourmet, but Max likes it, and there's plenty. And I can add garlic bread and a salad and turn it into a special occasion."

There was that smile again, the one she couldn't resist. But she had to. Because there was one insurmountable fact here that she wouldn't challenge in any way… Dermott needed his time with Max. And Max needed that time, probably even more than Dermott did. If anybody understood the hell that a child of an addicted parent suffered, she did. And while Max was still so young, the indelible impression was there. Dermott did have to protect that little boy and she had no place interfering. "Thanks, but I don't think so. Not tonight." A good salad from the diner would be fine, then a walk afterwards would top off the evening nicely.

Yes, that salad did hit the spot an hour later. The diner was bustling, and she felt almost guilty taking up a whole booth just for herself when so many people were standing in line, waiting for a seat. People she recognized now. Many of whom waved. It was like the diner where her grandparents used to take her—not so much in looks but in the friendliness. She used to love going there, used to love looking over the menu when all she ever ordered was a cheeseburger and a soda. And onion rings. "Sadie," she called as the waitress bustled past her. "Do you have onion rings here?"

"With your salad?" the young woman asked, probably wondering why anybody would ruin a healthy meal with a greasy follow-up.

Lately, though, she'd been thinking about her grandparents, wondering how they were. Little things, like the chocolate-chip cookies Max's grandmother made for him reminded her of the sugar cookies her own grandmother had made for her. So many things in Fort Dyott reminded her of the years she'd lived with them. Good years in so many ways, but that had been so long ago, and she had so many regrets. "Yes. Onion rings with my salad. You don't happen to have sugar cookies on the menu too, do you?"

The onion rings were delicious, but not as good as the ones she remembered. Then, after a brisk pace up one side of the main street then back down the other, Jenna was debating whether or not to expand her hiking horizons over another couple blocks, or go home and curl with up a good romance novel, when her cellphone rang. "Jenna Lawson," she answered, curious about the incoming number. She didn't recognize it.

"We have an emergency out at the Charney ranch," the voice on the other end stated. "Joshua Charney may have a broken leg."

"Who is this?" she asked.

"Lee Rodgers, ma'am. I'm the police chief in Fort Dyott."

"So tell me about Joshua."

"He's six years old, ma'am. And not responding so well. He's breathing too fast. I tried to take a pulse on him and it seems fast, too. He's also pretty pale."

"Is he crying?"

"No, ma'am. More like he's staring at the wall."

Going into shock? "Have you contacted Dermott yet?"

"Can't do that, ma'am."

"But the boy needs a doctor."

Rather than arguing with Jenna, Lee Rodgers told her how to get to the ranch, then hung up. And didn't answer when she tried the redial, so she called Dermott.

"Callahan," he answered.

His voice was lazy, deep. So sexy it gave her shivers. "We have an emergency. Child named Joshua Charney. Broken leg, maybe. I think it could be serious, judging from the way the police chief described it."

"Then they'll be taking him over to Muledeer. Alisa Charney was Nancy's best friend, and she won't speak to me."

"No. They want me out there right now, and I'm not so sure I should be going alone on this one. I can patch scratches and apply ointment, but if this is a compound fracture..." She reached the door to the clinic at the exact same time Dermott opened it for her. "If they've called the police, I'm assuming it's serious," she said, still speaking into her phone even though they were practically face to face now.

He handed her a medical bag, and she noticed he carried one, too.

She tucked her phone into her pocket. "What about Max?"

"Frank and Irene will watch him. It's on the way."

Max came out the door after Dermott, his face covered with orange spaghetti sauce. "Good color," she said, as the boy climbed into Dermott's truck. "Might look good to match that color as an accent to some of the blue and purple in your bedroom."

Max regarded a spot of it on his shirt and gave Jenna a thumbs-up sign as Dermott climbed into the driver's seat. "Aren't you getting in?" Dermott asked her.

"I'll take my car. That'll cut off a few minutes while you drop off Max."

"The road's tricky out there. Several turns, without road signs. You'll get lost." He pulled Max closer to him then gestured to the empty seat. "It's going to take a good fifteen minutes as it is, and I'm not waiting for you to keep up."

Rather than arguing the point, Jenna jumped in and they were already flying down the road by the time she got her door shut and locked. Dermott was on the phone to his father-in-law, telling him to be ready for Max, before she'd fastened her seat belt. "Do you know Joshua?" she asked.

"He and Max used to play together. He's bigger than Max, though. Big for his age and people forget he's only six."

"He likes soccer," Max chimed in. "We used to be on the same team. He was the captain."

"You aren't on the same team now?"

"I don't play any more, but I used to like it." Sad words from a little boy who seemed to want to play.

"Why don't you play?" Jenna asked before she caught Dermott's scowl.

"The big guy says I don't have time," Max said stiffly. "My grandpa needs me more."

Dermott *was* over-protective, pulling Max out of soccer. It struck Jenna that the boy needed a little normalcy in his life. Of course, that was none of her business. "Grandpas are the important people," Jenna said. "My grandpa is."

"Because he has horses," Max stated, quite emphatically. "Do you help him?"

"I used to."

"Did you have fun, because I would if I could help your grandpa."

"Fun" was such an ill-sorted word. When she'd helped her grandfather tend the horses there'd been nothing at all fun about it. It had only become fun later, in her memories. "Yes, I *did* have fun, Max. Quite a lot of fun, actually."

"And I can ride one there someday and have fun, too." He nudged his dad in the ribs. "Will you take me there when I'm taller, big guy?"

"How about we talk about it *when* you're taller?"

Max pulled a pouty face over that answer and slumped down in the seat, arms folded across his chest, his head down. Jenna couldn't help but feel sorry for him as it seemed his life was only a shuttle between his dad and his grandparents, with nothing in between. No other stops, no friends. At some point Dermott would let up, but right now there was a little boy who desperately needed to do some little-boy things, and her heart went out to him because he was too young to understand Dermott's fierce need to take care of him.

After they dropped Max off with his grandparents, the next five minutes passed in silence. "I don't always get it right," he finally said.

"You mean with Max? I think you're being a very good father."

"I know I'm smothering him."

"Which is natural. I think it's probably a little self-protection for the both of you, so don't be so hard on yourself. Things will eventually get back to normal."

"Normal…whatever that is."

"Maybe soccer again," she suggested. "If he wants to."

"But people talk, and I don't want him hearing what they might be saying. Not yet. Not until he's old enough to understand better."

"Don't underestimate him, Dermott. Children have this amazing way of understanding much more than we think they do." She laid a gentle hand on his arm. "And don't underestimate yourself either, because you'll know when it's time to let go a little. If you don't, I have an idea Max will let you know."

"When did you get so smart about children, JJ? I live with one and don't have a clue, and you…"

"I have all kinds of advice without having any practical experience." Except she'd lived the life, fought the battles, done everything wrong. If there was one lesson she'd learned over the years, it was that experience was the very best teacher.

"You told me not to underestimate myself, but maybe that's what I should be telling you, because even if you don't have a lot of experience, you've got good instinct, and a nice ability with children. A great empathy for them. I think Max senses that, too. You'd be a good mother."

"I don't think so. It's easy standing on the outside, looking in…giving unsolicited advice. But there are so many ways to mess up as a parent, and with the way I stumble through life, I'd be bound to go wrong in some pretty bad ways. I love children, but they're just not for me."

"You'll change your mind."

"I don't think so, not with the patterns I seem destined to repeat in my life."

"Then it's a pity, JJ, because I think you have an uncanny way of knowing what Max is feeling even better than I do."

"I just put myself in his place." Something she could do so well.

"Which is why you know he wants to go back to soccer."

"Well, that one's pretty obvious." She laughed. "And I have an idea that you'll be hearing his opinion on the subject from time to time."

"Time to time? More like minute to minute."

"So you'll let him?"

"It's nice that you're such an advocate, JJ. Max needs that from someone besides his grandparents and me. So, let's just say that I'll think about it."

"For a five-year-old, thinking about it is the same as saying no. You do realize that, don't you?"

"I wish Max's mother had been on his side, the way you are." Dermott let out a deep sigh, then changed the subject. "It's around the next corner. And let me warn you that Alisa Charney won't be friendly to me. She won't even want me in her house."

"Because she was Nancy's friend?"

"Because she blamed me for Nancy's problems, and her death."

She wanted to ask more, but he swerved around a curve in the road a little too fast and the truck spun tires on the dirt road. "That's it, straight ahead," he said. "And just so you'll know, I'll go in, but Alisa will refuse to let me see Joshua, so while I'm trying to convince her that I've got to take a look at him, you go on in and start the diagnosis, get his vital signs, make all the necessary assessments. I don't want to waste any time on this, and Alisa's going to be pretty fierce at protecting her son from me."

"That doesn't make sense."

"She accused me of neglecting my wife, JJ. She said that if I'd paid more attention, Nancy wouldn't have… Nancy was like a sister to her, and I don't want to subject Alisa to any more grief than she's already been though."

This wasn't easy for Dermott, none of it was. It seemed like life was slamming down on him from every direction and he was so good about dealing with it. Her solution was to simply run away when life got tough, and she truly wished she had some of his determination. "My orthopedic experience is pretty limited, but I'll do the best I can." It was nice to be trusted, and even nicer that Dermott was the one trusting her.

When they pulled into the driveway at the Charney house, every light inside the house was lit, and to someone passing by it might have appeared that they were having a party or family reunion inside that quaint little house. What Jenna found when she entered was anything but that, however. Joshua Charney was indeed large for his age. He could have passed for two or three years older than his six years. But he was every bit a six-year-old boy, and as Jenna bent over his bed to check his broken leg, what she discovered was that he was a critically ill six-year-old boy with serious compromise, and a home-made treatment that could do further damage. His leg was wrapped, elevated, had ice on the swelling. All the worst things to do if what she suspected turned out to be the case…things she immediately corrected. "I need Dermott in here," she yelled to the people in the hall.

"That man's not going near my son!" Alisa physically stepped into the doorway to prevent Dermott from entering. Her brother, the sheriff, took the same stance directly behind her.

"Is it compartmentalized?" Dermott asked from the hall. "Can you tell, Jenna?"

"I think it is. His blood pressure's low, his pulse fast and thready." She turned away from Joshua to face his mother. "How long as he been going in and out of consciousness?"

"He's sleeping!" she defended. "A couple of hours now."

"Dermott, he's not sleeping," Jenna said, bending over the boy to check the pupils in his eyes. She flashed a light directly in and looked for changes. Then moved the light back and forth to see if his eyes followed it. What she saw wasn't good. The boy did have a sluggish response to the light, but he wasn't rousing the way he should.

"Dermott," she called, "he's non-responsive, and my best guess is that he's either suffered internal injuries his parents don't know about, or it's compartmental syndrome, like you suspected." Which meant the swelling was literally cutting off circulation to the bone and, effectively, killing it. Either way this played out, this boy needed a doctor. "Your son needs Dr. Callahan," she said to Mrs. Charney.

"If he needs a doctor, we'll take him over to Muledeer, if that's what we have to do. They have a nice clinic there, and—"

"The drive will hurt him even more." Jenna hated being blunt but she was left with no recourse. Alisa Charney was a fierce woman when it came to her son's care. In this case, though, fierce wasn't good.

"I'll take care of him, Alisa," Dermott practically whispered.

"The way you took care of Nancy?" She shook her head frantically and clamped both her hands to the doorframe. "No!" she wailed. "I won't let you!"

Jenna knew Alisa Charney wasn't a bad mother. Just a very frightened one. Nothing in their house gave her any reason to believe that the Charneys weren't anything but good parents. Except they were stubborn and misguided which, in the end, would hurt their son. So she had to get through to them. "He needs a doctor now, and he's in no shape for a two-hour drive to Muledeer." Jenna turned her next plea to Joshua's father, a big, burly man with much kinder eyes than his wife's. "No matter how careful you are driving him to Muledeer, Mr. Charney, you're going to put your son at risk. Right now he's in critical condition and he needs Dermott to take care of him. It's about Joshua, not about your wife's feelings about

Dermott." She lowered her voice. "And your wife's feelings, Mr. Charney, could kill your son."

That had the impact she needed because Ron Charney looked like he'd been slapped. "Do what you need to, Dermott. I don't have a fight with you, and I'm trusting you to help my boy."

"No!" Alisa wailed. She spun around to her husband. "How could you?"

In that moment Dermott brushed past her and went straight to the bed where Joshua was now experiencing compromised breathing. He was struggling for air, no doubt effecting the blood-gas balances. "I've got emergency oxygen in the truck, behind the seat," he told Jenna. "And have the sheriff call Edmonton for air transport. We need to get Joshua into a major trauma center as soon as possible."

Meanwhile, Alisa crumpled into Ron's arms and was weeping, and Ron was saying something to her in quiet tones as he stroked her hair. Jenna's heart went out to them as she ran past, so she stopped for a moment. "I know it's not an easy thing for you to do, letting Dermott take care of your son, but he's a good doctor, Alisa. Deep down I think you know that or else you'd have already taken Joshua to Muledeer. I'm sorry for your loss with Nancy, but please understand that Dermott and I will do whatever's necessary here, and if I had a son there's no doctor in the world I'd trust him to as much as I would Dermott."

"Then you don't know him," Alisa snapped.

"Actually, I do. For a very long time now." That's where she left it, as Alisa pulled away from her husband and ran into the bedroom to stand over Dermott's shoulder. Within another few minutes Jenna had oxygen on the boy, and Dermott was in the process of inserting an IV. Thank goodness, Alisa had stepped back to allow them to do their job.

He was taking another blood-pressure reading, trying to fight back the anger. What were these people thinking? That he'd hurt Joshua, or do something medically wrong on purpose? "How long has he been this way?" he called out to nobody in particular. "Tell me how he was injured."

"About four hours total now," Ron said. The man stepped into the doorway, filling up most of it, and had to grab hold for support when he saw the hard way his son's chest was lurching now. "He got his leg caught in the tractor wheel. Don't know how. Didn't even know he was playing out there until I heard the screaming."

"When did he start having problems?" Dermott asked.

"Not for a little while. He was crying, but I didn't see any blood. I thought it might be broken, but I figured that could keep until we could get over to the clinic in Muledeer tomorrow…" He broke off, sucked in a sharp breath. "You know how it is, Doc. I would have called about this, but Alisa still has some mighty strong feelings."

Dermott didn't acknowledge that verbally, but he nodded, extending a half-smile to the man. Compartmental syndrome, without a doubt. Of all the bad luck for the boy! It made Dermott want to go home and hold Max for the rest of the night. "Lee," he called to the sheriff. "When you arrange for the air transport, tell them to expect a compartment fracture." And possible amputation if they didn't do something fast.

"But no internal injuries?" Jenna asked Dermott.

"I don't think so. I think it's just his leg." He lowered his voice. "We may need to do a fasciotomy, right here, though. Could you start to prep the area? I have gauze, but not enough antiseptic."

"That bad?" she whispered.

He nodded. "We're out of time. They waited so long…" He turned to Ron as Jenna took some gauze pads from his medical bag and went running to the bathroom to look for some kind of antiseptic agent—alcohol, peroxide, anything to sterilize the area. "So after you found Joshua with his leg caught in the tire, what happened next?"

"Brought him into the house, did some first-aid things. You know, the regular kind…elevated his leg, put ice on it, wrapped it up."

Dear God! Wrapping the leg kept the swelling compressed, which was the first worst thing that could happen because it put undue pressure on the nerves and blood vessels. The second worst thing was elevating it when what his leg really needed was to stay level with the heart so the heart wouldn't strain so much in pumping blood to it. To a leg that was literally starving for that blood circulation, depriving it in any way could result in amputation. Dermott did an immediate probe of the injured area and winced. There was a tight feel to the muscle compartment there. Too tight. "When did you remove the wrap and quit elevating his leg?"

"Your nurse did, the minute she came into the room. She took one look and pulled it off. Was that a bad thing? Did she hurt my boy doing that?"

"No. She probably saved his leg." That impressed him. Jenna had good instincts. He'd always admired that in her but, to be honest, back in the day he'd been admiring, it hadn't been focused so much on her medical skills. He glanced up at her as she came running into the room with a bottle of rubbing alcohol, amazed even more that in the middle of so much turmoil this one bright spot had come into his life.

"Like I figured, the muscle compartment's constricted," he whispered to her. "And since Joshua's not conscious I can't evaluate his sensation. Which puts us in a bad position here." The fasciotomy he was about to do would remove the fascia, a thin connective tissue covering, or separating, the muscles and internal organs of the body. The procedure was a relatively simple one, although not done outside the operating theater too often. "If we wait much longer he loses a leg. Yet if we risk an emergency procedure here you know what that could turn into if something goes bad, and we don't have the proper equipment."

Jenna sucked in a sharp breath and held it a moment before letting it out. "I'm ready."

"You're not going to argue me out of it?" he asked, half-teasing.

"I think you'll get enough of that from everybody else." She nodded toward the door where the Charneys, as well as the police chief, were all glaring at them. "Look, Dermott. How about I go deal with the people while you get him ready?"

"I really should have paid more attention to your medical skills back when we were…well, whatever the hell it was we were."

She laughed. "Well, as it turned out, I paid attention to *your* medical skills back then, but I was paying attention to something else even more." She reached over and gave his hand an affectionate squeeze, then went to face off with the people who would in no way want Dermott taking a knife to Joshua.

Funny how some things worked out, he thought. Maybe more like, amazing. Or meant to be?

"There's no other choice," Jenna said, after her third attempt to explain the procedure to Joshua's parents. She *had* to get their permission, or Dermott couldn't start.

"There's one," Alisa snapped. "And that's to wait for the air transport. Because I'm not letting that man cut my son. I let him take a look and now he wants to operate?" She gave her husband a pleading look. "We can't do that, Ron. We can't let him."

"Why do you hate him so much?" Jenna asked. "He's in there, trying to save your boy's leg, and maybe his life, yet you hate him so much you're not being rational about this."

"Oh, I'm being rational," the other woman argued. "Protecting my son from a man like that is being very rational."

"He can't wait. If Dermott says—"

"If Dermott says…" Alisa mocked. "I've heard what

Dermott says, and it killed my best friend. How can you ask me to trust someone like that?"

Jenna's heart went out to her, and given any other circumstance she would have backed off, but right now she couldn't do that. Dermott was ready to start, and Joshua wasn't getting any better. Sure, it was a judgment call, but most emergency procedures were. So it all came down to trust, and she trusted Dermott. Implicitly. She reached out and took hold of Alisa's trembling hand. "I understand your conflicts with Dermott. You loved Nancy, and she died, and you blame Dermott for that.

"Blame him? I accuse him!"

Jenna lowered her voice. "Because his wife got herself addicted to drugs?"

"Because he didn't know. If anyone should have seen what was happening…"

Jenna understood that. Alisa was hurt. Angry. She blamed herself because a best friend should have noticed, and she took it out on Dermott because a husband should have noticed too. It was all so sad and there was always so much blame to go around when none was deserved. Hadn't she blamed herself when she'd been abused? And hidden her own truths so very well, concealing the bruises her father had left after he'd hit her? Hadn't she done a fine job of applying make-up to the tell-tale evidence and wearing long sleeves even in the sweltering heat, then explaining away the odd attire quite convincingly?

Yes, she understood, and she did feel sorry for Alisa. But people who didn't want to be found out went to extraordinary lengths to hide the truth. Jenna had. So had Nancy Callahan.

"Dermott should have known!" Alisa snarled. "He should have…" There were no more words for Alisa. Her anger was white hot and so painful Jenna doubted it would be quelled for a long, long time.

Jenna sighed, fighting to stay calm. "Look, Alisa. Don't let your feelings for Dermott get in the way of what he's trying to do for Joshua. Your son needs this procedure right now if he's going to have any chance at all of keeping his leg."

"I don't know," Alisa sobbed. She looked up at her husband for help, then went limp and collapsed in his arms.

"Just do it," Ron said, still not looking at Jenna. "Just do whatever the hell you have to do to help my boy." He pulled Alisa even closer to his huge barrel chest, and she looked dwarfed against the large man. "It's our son, for God's sake, Alisa! I know you hate Dermott, but he's the only one here who can do this." Together, Alisa and Ron turned away from Jenna as she rushed back into the bedroom to take Dermott's side. The hatred ran so deep it was virulent. And sad for everyone.

"Good to go," she said, and without reply Dermott made his incision over the swollen area of Joshua's leg, cut through the fatty tissue, the surgery commenced.

"None of it's necrotic yet," Dermott said, on a sigh of relief. Meaning the leg wasn't yet dying for a lack of blood. "Although the compromise is pretty pronounced. But I think we might get lucky here and this boy will keep his leg."

"How long before it would have gone necrotic?" she asked, as she retracted the edges of skin while Dermott continued his work.

"Hard to say. Maybe as long as an hour, or just a few more minutes. He was getting pretty close to the point where we couldn't have corrected the compromise."

"He wouldn't have made it to the hospital, then." And Joshua's chances of keeping his leg would have been practically non-existent. Dermott was so good, and she wanted Alisa to acknowledge that, but to Dermott it was all about the work, about taking care of the patient, not the accolades that should have gone with it. Still, it hurt her that Dermott was so despised by that woman. It made her feel sad, too.

Once he'd cut all the way through the fatty layer, Dermott

removed a tiny piece of the fascia, just enough to let the swelling expand to relieve the pressure, then he swabbed the area with sterile gauze, bandaged it, and they were done. He pulled off his surgical gloves, tossed them into a trash can at the side of Joshua's bed, and simply took a blood-pressure reading like this was any other routine physical.

"Better," he said, pulling the stethoscope from his ears.

"That was amazing, Dermott."

He shrugged, trying to be modest, but his eyes fairly sparkled with the success as he continued to do the routine assessments—pulse, pupils, blood pressure again. And maybe that's when she knew… In just that tiniest moment when the realization that Joshua Charney was going to be up and playing with the other little boys again, another realization hit her that maybe, just maybe, she was falling a little bit in love with Dermott. It wouldn't work, of course, and she'd never admit it aloud, but a tiny speck of her heart felt it. Just a tiny speck, that's all. At least, that's what she was telling herself when she went out to tell the Charneys the good news.

"Then it's over?" Alisa asked, rushing to her son's side and dropping to her knees to hug him.

"It's over," Dermott assured. "He'll be fine until we can get him to the hospital and fix his leg. What I did was just temporary."

"But enough that you don't need to do anything else to him?" Alisa asked.

"Nothing else, except watch him until the helicopter gets here."

"And your nurse can do that?"

"Yes," he said. "She can."

"Then I'll be asking you to leave, Dermott. You're not welcome in my house."

Jenna was too stunned to speak. Stunned not only by Alisa's cruelty toward a man who'd just saved her son's life, but by Dermott's reaction. He merely nodded, then packed his medical bag and walked out.

No one thanked him. No one acknowledged him. No one even looked at him. He simply took his medical bag, left the house, then he sat outside in front, in his truck, waiting, until the air transport arrived.

An hour later, after the police chief had gone his own way, Joshua had been packed into a helicopter and sent off to Edmonton, and his parents had taken to the road to drive there, nothing had changed. Not one single thing. Except on the trip back home there was no talk between the two of them. In fact, Dermott didn't say a word. Neither did Jenna, although she wanted to.

CHAPTER SIX

IT HAD been three days since they'd sent Joshua to hospital. Reports on his progress were encouraging and, in all likelihood, he'd be home within the week. So far Dermott hadn't spoken to Jenna about what had happened out at the Charney farm, and she hadn't mentioned it to him. For that matter, the Charneys had been strangely quiet, with not one word of gratitude forthcoming, which bothered her. Did it bother Dermott, too? If it did, he didn't let on. When people approached him, giving him that congratulatory slap on the back for saving Joshua Charney's life, and when Mrs. Brighton baked a cake and brought it in because somebody needed to bake a cake for such an occasion, Dermott was all smiles and charm. But when the door shut to those people, she saw it on his face...the strain, the frustration. There wasn't a thing she could do about it because Dermott shrugged it off...shrugged her off when she tried approaching him.

So she let it be. Still sometimes she had to fight off the desire to slip her arms around him.

Over the days, patients had come and gone in the clinic, enough so that Jenna was honestly encouraged about the practice in general, and about the practice's ability to support a nurse. That was good, because at times she really wanted to stay...for a while. No thoughts on permanence, naturally, but she could see herself fitting into an extended stay. Especially now that she was convinced there was a real need for her. Unfortunately, that tended to work as a double-edged sword from time to time, as projecting herself into very much of a future did throw her into a panic. So much so that she'd gone and packed, then unpacked, then packed her undies a time or two or three. Right now they were in the drawer, but the drawer was standing wide open just in case.

That morning, Jenna was tending to an early pregnancy, routine exam. The patient, Lolly Olsen, had purposely scheduled her appointment during the time Dermott went off for peanut butter sandwiches with Max. She claimed she'd rather be seen by a woman, but Jenna knew better. "I'm feeling great," she said, even though she seemed rather nervous. "No morning sickness. No weight gain yet."

"No unusual symptoms?" Jenna asked. Blood pressure was perfect, and everything checked out as it should.

"No, not really. It's just that…" She drew in a deep breath. "My age. It's got me worried."

"Your age?" Jenna checked the chart. Her patient was forty-three and this was her first pregnancy.

"You know, all the risk factors at my age. I don't want to bother Dermott, seeing what he's going through himself, because I'm probably being silly about it."

"Being worried isn't being silly," Jenna said. "And there are tests that can be done to determine how things are progressing with your pregnancy, and to make sure there aren't any genetic defects. We can also find out the sex of your baby, if you want to know. We're not equipped to do all that here, though, so you'll probably have to go to one of the larger cities…"

"That's not a problem. My mother lives in Calgary and I can go stay with her there for a while."

"Then I'll have Dr. Callahan write the orders, and we'll get things set up for you." Dermott had actually made those notes in the chart last time he'd seen Lolly, stating that she was due for a whole battery of tests after this visit. "And Lolly, forty-three isn't too old to be having a baby any more. Women are doing it well into their forties now, without bad consequences. You're healthy, everything checks out fine…"

"Have you had children?" she asked.

Jenna Lawson, mother. The thought had always been pushed out by more practical aspects like how she could barely manage her own life. "No children. I'm a career girl all the way."

"Me too, until this. I'm Fort Dyott's only dentist, and I'd given up trying to get pregnant years ago." She patted her flat belly. "Look at me now. It changes everything, you know. It's like I'm still the dentist during the day but I can't wait until I get home so I can bask in my pregnancy, eat pregnant-healthy foods, look at baby catalogs, go online to baby Web sites. And I think that once the baby arrives I'll probably find another dentist to take over my practice, or do what Dermott's doing and cut my patient load way back so I can spend as much time with my child as possible. However it works out, I don't want to miss a minute of my child growing up. My husband and I have waited too long for this and now that's it actually happening to us, we want to make sure we do everything right."

What an awesome thing to be happening to someone who wanted it so badly, Jenna thought several hours later, after the clinic had closed for the day. She was out for a late afternoon stroll, enjoying the warm weather, glad for the fresh air, mulling over the whole new life in store for the town's dentist. She envied Lolly a little. Her life had been set for such a long time, yet she was so excited to make a change for something so important, so wonderful. Having a baby… Jenna loved babies, loved children, loved the whole growing-up process, and at times she did think she might be a good mother. But other times, thinking like that caused her to break out in a cold sweat, caused her hands to shake, gave her a good bout of nausea. Not because she didn't love children, but because, in reality, she didn't love herself being involved with a child.

But for Lolly, she was happy. So happy in fact, that she ducked into a little boutique and bought the cutest pair of white baby booties for her.

Exiting the shop, she continued down the main street, window-shopping mostly. She liked Fort Dyott and, surprisingly, it had a nice little downtown area, with a pleasant variety of shops along a cobbled, tree-lined walkway. She could be happy here, she thought as she gazed into the ice-cream shop, and decided to go in for a treat. Inside, the shop was filled with cozy booths and tables, and Jenna carried her order of a double dip of peppermint ice cream to the booth nearest the window, where she settled in to eat it. But before she'd even had so much as her first bite raised to her lips, bits and pieces of a conversation from another booth behind her wafted over.

"It's good that he's getting his life back to normal now, what with the way Nancy went off and killed herself like she did," the first woman said.

"And the way she almost killed Max…" the second one responded.

Sadie, the waitress in the diner, had hinted that it hadn't been an overdose, and now that was confirmed. And whatever had happened had involved Max. That thought turned her stomach, causing her to push her ice cream away.

She understood how Dermott couldn't talk about it, and the more she learned, the more she sympathized. But it did bother her that he didn't trust her enough to tell her the whole story, and that she had to pick up bits and pieces of it in town, the way he'd predicted she might.

Admittedly, it hurt a little, being left out, because she trusted Dermott, and she was afraid he didn't trust her. Which was understandable, with her history of moving from place to place. It was probably his defense mechanism, something to keep him from getting too close, too personal. And just when she'd convinced herself that a few expectations here were OK.

No expectations, Jenna. That was the only thing that worked for her. So why couldn't she stick to that?

Jenna sat for another few minutes, watching the ice cream as it melted into a puddle in the bottom of the bowl, scolding herself mentally for falling a little in love with Dermott again, and for developing feelings for Fort Dyott. This wasn't her life here. She was merely a traveler passing through, and dreams of anything else would just make her time here miserable. Therefore, no more dreams. Easy as that. She'd put all the silly notions right out of her head, do her job, keep to herself. Which meant having nothing to do with Dermott outside the office. Which meant nothing in particular to look forward to. Or she'd leave if she couldn't do it.

That depressing thought slapped her hard, brought sharp tears to her eyes—tears she refused to spill in public, so she slipped out of the booth, then ran the full three blocks back to the clinic, hoping the exercise would knock the dreams and expectations out of her system. She didn't even remember running all the way from the ice-cream parlor when she flew through the front door and continued straight up the stairs. At the first landing, she paused just enough to catch her breath, then slowed her pace up the next flight. By the time she was at her own door, she was feeling stupid, overreacting the way she had. The truth was, nothing in Dermott's personal life should matter, and that included what he had told her, or hadn't told her, about *anything*. That it *did* matter so much was her greater concern here.

"You run good for a girl," Max said. He was standing half a flight down from her, with an expression on his face that clearly showed he wasn't sure what to do.

"You saw me running?"

He nodded. "The big guy and I were buying shoes." To show her, he held up his right foot to show off the brand-new pair of red canvas sneakers.

"So, where is the big guy?" She looked further down but

didn't see Dermott. What had he done? Sent Max up to see what was wrong with her?

"He's getting ready to go."

"Go where?" Jenna asked. "Another house call?"

"To take me back Grandma and Grandpa's. I'm going to spend the night there, and help Grandpa do some more painting, so he's packing my clothes. I need lots of them since I get all painty when I work."

In spite of the lousy way she'd just been feeling, Max made her smile. What a great kid! If there were any guarantees that she could have a child just like him, maybe she would. "Not in your new shoes, I hope. You could get blue paint on them, and the paint won't come out."

Max frowned for a moment, considering what she'd just said, then turned and tramped back down the stairs. She listened until he slammed their apartment door before she went inside her own. It wasn't but a minute until someone knocked on her door, and before she'd even crossed back over to open it, Dermott was calling, "Jenna, can I come in?"

"Why not?" she shouted, showing no enthusiasm whatsoever. He was going to ask her to cover the clinic while he was out, which was fine since her new resolve was work and nothing else.

"Look, Max and I are going out to the farm, and I was wondering..."

"Sure. Whatever." She didn't even look at him.

"Ten minutes, OK?"

"Fine. Oh, and just so you'll know, I've decided to find another place to live. It's not working out here in the apartment." She wasn't sure where that had come from since she hadn't really given it any thought, but it did seem like a good idea. And a sensible one, if she wanted to stay in Fort Dyott.

Well, if nothing else, it was a step in the right direction. Get out, get on. Wasn't that what she always did anyway?

"You always were a little stubborn and over-reactive, weren't you?"

"Over-reactive? What makes you think I'm over-reactive?"

"Weren't you reacting to something a little while ago, running like that? Then announcing you're moving out? You've always been impulsive, JJ, and you can't deny it."

"I can't, and I won't. It's the way I live my life, and I don't have to defend myself to you, Dermott. Not to you, or anybody."

"Whoa," he said, reaching out to take her arm. But she yanked away from him. "What's this about? Did I do something to make you angry, or hurt you? Or did someone else say something?"

"It's nothing you need to be bothered with," she said, her voice so stiff a good hard breeze would have snapped it in two. "We all deserve our privacy, don't we? Deserve the right to invite people into it, or exclude them. I respect that, and I hope you do, too."

"I know you're struggling here, Jenna. I didn't mean for that to happen, and I'm sorry it is. So is there anything I can do to help you?"

She shook her head no. In all honesty, the problem was with her, not him. So it was up to her to solve it. "Look, I'm fine. So why don't you two just go have a good time, and I'll call you if I need you."

"No need to call. I thought you might like to come with us. That's what this is, Jenna. An invitation for a ride while I take Max out to his grandparents. That's all."

Her first impulse was to accept it, but her newfound resolve tamped that back. "I have some reading to catch up on, and I thought I'd send out a few e-mails tonight, too. I appreciate the offer, but you two go on without me. I'd rather be alone this evening."

Rather than trying to argue her out of her decision, which she'd hoped he might do, Dermott merely nodded, then ran down the stairs. A minute later she heard the muffled "We're leaving" from the first floor, then she got her wish. She was alone. Just her, and the can of soup she intended to open for her dinner. And it was so lonely there.

"I need your help downstairs," Dermott yelled. "Front of the clinic, *stat*."

It hadn't even been an hour. She'd heated the tomato soup, eaten half of it, picked up a journal to read, then answered the phone. "On my way," she said, pulling on her shoes, heading for the stairs. So, what had he come across that had brought him right back to the clinic?

When Jenna reached the bottom stair and rounded the corner to the clinic waiting room, what she saw there wasn't an emergency. It was Dermott filling up the doorframe, a blanket tucked under one arm and a couple of pillows in the other. "What's this?" she demanded, even though the grin on his face was pretty revealing. He had plans for her.

"A picnic."

"I don't do picnics."

"Sure you do. Everybody does picnics."

Jenna shook her head. "You and Max go and have a good time. I, um...I have the rest my dinner waiting for me upstairs." Half a bowl of stone-cold soup.

"And I have dinner waiting for us in the truck. The two of us...you and me, not Max and me. And I promise, it's not peanut butter and jelly."

"You really know how to woo a girl, don't you?"

Dermott laughed. "Look. I know you haven't been having any fun here. Work is slower than you're used to, I'm tied up with Max every minute I'm not working. And I'm sorry about that, JJ. It wasn't fair of me to invite you here and strand you the way I have."

"You're not forcing me to stay, Dermott."

"Maybe not, but I do have some responsibility in it, and I want to make it better for you here."

"With a picnic?"

He nodded. "With a picnic. Maybe a couple hours away will do you some good. Make you smile like you actually mean it. You know, be happy here, because I don't think you are."

"I want to be happy, Dermott. I want to like Fort Dyott, and my job here. I want to fall in love with all the small-town charm and eat peppermint ice cream in a parlor where they're not talking about…" She cut it off. Sighed stiffly, quite surprised she had so many wishes to spill out. "This is the side of me you didn't know about, the one that gets restless and finds reasons to keep to myself, or even move on if I have to. I don't want to, but it's what I do. Which is crazy, because sometimes, when I'm feeling too settled or happy, it's like I can't get away fast enough."

"A self-defense mechanism. But what are you protecting yourself from, Jenna? For me, it's rumors and speculations and people who mean well but don't know better and might say something to Max I don't want him to hear."

"For me, it's…me. I'm just not good over the very long haul." She laughed, but it was filled with so much sadness. "So I don't get involved in anything other than my work. It's just easier that way."

"That's because you resign yourself to baby steps when you could be taking big leaps."

"Baby steps work for me. They're safe."

"Do they, though? You've convinced yourself that's what you want because it's safe, but deep down, JJ, that's not you. You're the kind of person who should be breaking free of those baby steps and taking big, huge leaps because that's what's in you. It was there all those years ago, and it still is. But you fight it."

Jenna swallowed hard. She desperately wanted him to be right about that. All those big leaps got too complicated, and took her to places she didn't belong. The baby steps were safer. Sure, they might not take her far, but at this point in her life, the trade-off was fine—relative safety over almost anything else. "You know what, Dermott? I think you should be getting back to Max now. He's probably wondering where you are."

He gave her a curious look like he wasn't ready to end the conversation, then he must have changed his mind because his expression switched from serious to a mischievous twinkle, with a playful arch of his left eyebrow. "Actually, Max helped pack the picnic basket, and he was pretty insistent it had to be for the two of *us*. You don't want to disappoint him, do you?"

Was there a hidden agenda in there somewhere? Or was this Dermott simply taking pity on her and trying to be kind? With Dermott, it was hard to tell. "And what would I be getting myself into with this picnic?"

"It's a no-strings-attached picnic down at the river. Beautiful sunset, one of the best in Alberta. Good food prepared by my own hand, if you don't mind tuna salad sandwiches and wine. Modestly pleasant company. Modestly pleasant conversation with that modestly pleasant company. Modestly nice couple of hours away from everything. And did I mention, no strings attached?"

When he stood there grinning at her the way he was, it was hard to resist him. His picnic idea sounded nice, as a matter of fact. So maybe she shouldn't get all suspicious or cautious because it could be that a picnic was a picnic was a picnic, no agendas or pity intended. "You don't have to entertain me, Dermott. Like I said, I have plans for the evening that suit me just fine."

"Did it ever occur to you that I might want you to entertain me? You know, adult conversation, or medical conversation between two medical professionals."

"Which is it?"

"Some of it all. You need to get away. I need to get away. I need an hour or two where all the things that normally bother me won't bother me. So, do I have to beg?"

Jenna laughed, not at anything funny so much as that mischievous twinkle. He simply couldn't hide it. "OK, I hate seeing a grown man beg." She paused, faking a frown. "Were you going to get down on your knees?"

"Is that what you'd like to see?"

She never could win one of these little skirmishes with Dermott. In truth, she'd never really wanted to. "What if I said yes?" Keeping a straight face was a struggle, and she had to bite down on her lower lip to keep from smiling. "What if I told you that I'd love to see you down on your knees?"

"Only for a marriage proposal. And that, JJ, never comes before the tuna salad sandwich. So, go grab your sweater. Once the sun goes down, so does the temperature, and I'm not sure you're ready to have me keep you warm the only way I know how."

Jenna saw that mischievous twinkle again just as she turned to run and fetch her sweater. The thing was, he might have only been teasing, but common sense was reminding her that a sunset picnic with Dermott had played into a fantasy or two in the past. In fact, hadn't she once told him that her idea of the most romantic date in the world was a sunset picnic, with a nice bonfire and a cozy soft blanket?

Had he remembered that? Like the ice cream, the tea, her birthday? The coincidences were adding up, weren't they?

Dear lord, she didn't want to think about that! But the more she didn't want to, the more she did.

The chat between the two of them was casual as they drove away from town. Some of it entailed the medical practice, most of it was about Max. All safe ground, and she was glad for that because it put the notion of romance further out of her head. Where it belonged.

Just getting out of Fort Dyott had such a calming effect— or maybe that calming effect came from being with Dermott— she didn't want to disrupt that in any way. So they talked, and

Jenna also took a good bit of time to stare at the magnificent sights out the window. Alberta's landscape in this area was stunning. She hadn't paid much attention on her way in, but on this little byway they were traveling, where the flat plains opened into a craggy expanse of hills and forest, the perfect composure of it all simply flowed into her, making her feel at peace, helping her understand why Dermott wanted to come here. He needed that tranquility even more than she did.

"It's a hidden gem," he said, as they hiked their way through a woody patch, up the side of a modest hill. "I used to like coming here when…" He broke off.

When what? When he and Nancy had been married? Was he actually bringing her to the place he'd brought his wife? Jenna stopped cold in her tracks. "When what, Dermott?" she demanded.

He spun around to face her. "When I was a boy. We lived near here for a little while, and this is where I came when I ran away from home for a few days."

"I thought…"

"I know what you thought…that I used to bring my wife here. That's right, isn't it?"

"What else was I supposed to think?"

"That maybe I'd have enough sense not to bring someone I care for to a place I'd brought my wife."

He looked hurt, but he turned away from her so quickly she couldn't tell for sure. "Why do you always do that? Just walk away from it? Or ignore it?" Where was the old Dermott? She'd started out on this picnic with him, but he'd disappeared somewhere along the way, and she wanted him back. Desperately.

"What I do, Jenna, is what I think is best for everyone involved. I've had so much confrontation, I just…" He shook his head in frustration. "It's not too far away. How about we continue there, spread out the blanket, have a nice meal, and then…" Shrugging, Dermott turned back to the trail and continued to walk, and they didn't say another word until they stopped at a spot that was so breathtaking all Jenna could do was stand and stare for a moment.

"You found this when you were a boy?" she asked.

"By accident. I'd heard about a higher bluff, one where you could look down and see some circular stone medicine wheels—they were used by the Blackfoot First Nation in spiritual rites and death ceremonies. I was the big-city boy who really wanted to see the Indian ruins, but the big-city boy had a pretty bad sense of direction, and this is where I ended up. Not that I'm complaining, because in time it became one of my favorite places in the world."

"I don't suppose I really have a favorite place," Jenna said, spreading out the blanket. It *was* soft and cozy. "And to be honest, most of my outdoor experience has been limited to city parks."

"You can have this. That is, if you want a favorite place."

Kneeling down on the blanket, she stared at Dermott, who'd already sprawled out. In the background, the rush of water over the river rocks seemed almost like a balm for all the anxieties she'd been feeling for so long. "You'd let me share it with you?"

"Or you can have it all to yourself, if that's what you want."

It was only a gesture, but it meant so much. The kindness, the sincerity…she hadn't felt those things from anybody in such a long time and when she looked into Dermott's eyes, that's what she saw. That, and so much more. "I think I'm tired of having things all to myself," she said, finally relaxing, finally trusting. It was difficult, trusting the old Dermott and having so many unanswered questions about the one who'd replaced him. It was her problem to deal with, though, and this was a start. At least, she wanted to make it a start, because there were so many qualities in the new Dermott she really did admire.

"You go through that phase in your life where it's good to

be independent. You have your own rules, you can tweak your life into anything you want it to be and there's no one there to be contrary or doubtful. But then you grow up…or, shall I say, grow wiser. The things that were essential in establishing yourself aren't important any more because you've achieved what you wanted toward that end, or mellowed enough that they don't matter any longer. Then, somewhere along the way, you get really tired of everything being about yourself. If you're single, it's hard to step out of that. If you're fortunate to have someone else, the way you have Max, the changes happen because you want them to happen, and all the things you've had to yourself become about someone who turns out to be the most important person in your life. Does that make sense?"

Dermott nodded. "I am fortunate. And you're right. My life is all about Max now. He *is* the most important person in my life. So, did you ever want children, Jenna? I mean, you're not too old, not even close to it. But have you ever thought about it?"

Since she'd bought those baby booties, she'd thought about that more than once. "I love children. They're these wonderful little bundles of energy and intelligence and insight that can amaze you and confuse you and scare you to death. But me as a mother…"

"You have a natural instinct, and Max responds to it. He really does like you, and that's a high compliment from a young man who hasn't had much womanly experience outside his grandmother and a couple of little girls in town his own age he'd rather hit than woo."

"But the hitting will turn into wooing."

"That's what I'm afraid of. Max, as a ladies' man."

"Like his father."

Dermott arched playful eyebrows. "And what do you mean by that?"

She arched playful eyebrows back at him. "I wasn't the only one you took to the supply closet."

"Where'd you ever hear something like that?"

"No one had to tell me. But I saw the way all the women reacted to you, and you saw it too. In fact, I'm pretty sure you were flattered by all the attention."

Pulling a bottle of chardonnay from the hamper, Dermott inserted the corkscrew and popped out the cork. "Of course I was flattered," he said, as he poured the wine into two stemmed goblets, then handed one to Jenna. "Any red-blooded man in my position would have been flattered. But being flattered and acting on it are two different things."

"So you're telling me I was the only one?"

"At the time, yes."

A straightforward answer, and it surprised her a little. Yet in a way, it didn't. Dermott was steady, he didn't play with people's emotions, didn't lead them on. Jenna lifted her glass. "Then, to old times. They weren't so bad."

He clinked his glass to hers. "Old times. They were pretty damned good, if you ask me." He took a sip, then studied her for a moment. "Would you have cared if you weren't the only one I took to the supply closet?"

"Maybe, a little." Dermott did have a bit of a bad-boy reputation back then, but that had all been part of the appeal. Would she have stayed with him, even for those few weeks, had she been one of his many? "Yes, I think I might have cared."

"Well, just so you'll know, you were the only one I ever took to *that* supply closet, or any other. Reputation or not, I was too busy working my way through med school and a residency to get myself involved. You were as close as I came. So why'd you run away after we got caught?"

"You scared me. I scared me. Everything scared me. I was seeing things in myself that didn't belong there…"

"Things I'd caused?" Dermott asked gently.

"Some of them. And when I realized how easy it was to get so out of control with you, I decided to get myself back under control. It was only a fling. We knew that at the start and I thought a clean break was for the best."

"Was it really only a fling, JJ? Because it seemed like so much more."

She paused, glass halfway to her lips, and frowned. "That's what it was supposed to be. What we'd agreed on, and I was sticking to our agreement." Lifting the glass the rest of the way to her lips, she took a large gulp of the wine, nearly emptying the glass. As he picked up the bottle to refill it, she refused. Getting light-headed from too much wine too fast wasn't what she wanted of this evening. Although…she truly didn't know what she did want. "I know it doesn't seem so from your perspective, but I keep a pretty tight rein on my life and when things get complicated, I uncomplicate them."

"By running away?"

"If that's what it takes. I can work anywhere, and there are a lot of sights to see." She didn't want this to be about her any more. Dermott was getting too close, asking questions that needed real answers, and she didn't want to lie to him. But she didn't want to tell him the truth, either. Didn't want to dig down to that place inside herself where the necessary answers were buried. It was too painful. "So, how long did you stay out here on your big adventure?"

"Just a couple of nights. I didn't plan my food situation very well, and since I don't hunt or fish, I decided that the home situation with food was probably better than the freedom situation without food. The hell of it was, nobody even mentioned my absence. Years later I learned that my dad had followed me, and stayed a way off watching me, making sure I was fine." He laughed. "Next time I ran away I took more food."

"But you went home again?"

"I always went home because home is home. It grounds you."

"And your parents…"

"Living in Costa Rica now. They wanted to retire to some-place warm all the time, so they're whiling away their retire-ment in a little cottage overlooking the beach. It's a good life, and a nice home there for the family, when we care to go and visit."

"You make a very nice home here for Max," she said.

"It's not enough. He has stability with his grandparents, much more than he has with me. And I always feel guilty that the structure of his life is so up and down. It always has been."

"Even with his mother, before she had problems?" She hadn't meant to ask, but it had just popped out. "I'm sorry, Dermott. I didn't mean…"

"No need to apologize for what's so obvious. Nancy was a good mother for a little while. She adored Max, loved dressing him up and taking him out, showing off all the cute little outfits she'd bought for him. But then one day she wasn't a good mother any longer. She hated the responsibilities. Hated being held down. Hated everything about it."

"What did you do?"

"My practice was busy and I couldn't take time off to watch Max, so Nancy's parents stepped in for me most of the time. And when they couldn't, a couple of the young girls in town were happy to help. It worked out, and Nancy didn't seem to mind the arrangement."

But Dermott had. She could see that written all over him—in the tight way he folded his arms across his chest, in the clenching of his jaw, the frown creasing his brow. "Many children are raised by caregivers these days. It works out."

His eyes softened for a moment as he looked over at her. "For Max, it was a blessing. A lot of people loved that little boy. A lot of people, except his mother." Then his eyes went black. "The big secret, Jenna. The one people whisper about but never quite say aloud… Nancy didn't just die of natural causes or an overdose, as you've probably already guessed. She killed herself. We were separated by then because I didn't trust her with Max. She went to her parents' house one day when they had him, took him away from them, put him in the car…" He swallowed hard. "She was high, according to the medical examiner. Don't know if she was when she went to Frank and Irene's, or if it happened afterwards. But she hit a pole. Didn't even put on her brakes when she was heading right at it."

"Max wasn't hurt?"

Dermott shook his head slowly. "Max wasn't hurt," he whispered, his voice wobbling. "But he was so frightened."

"Thank God he was safe." She scooted over close to Dermott, took his hand in hers. "It wasn't your fault," she said softly. "I know you blame yourself because you were working and not with Max when it happened, not there to stop Nancy from taking him, and I'm so sorry for everything that happened, but what counts is the way you're raising Max now. The rest is…over." Easy to say, not easy to take to heart, and she knew that better than anyone.

"I'd filed for divorce already. She wasn't happy with me, or with our life together, so I wanted to let her go and find whatever made her happy, and I never wanted her to…die. But she couldn't let go of…"

"Home," Jenna supplied. "Because home is home." It was a concept Jenna was only just now beginning to understand.

He sighed. "She hurt so many people here. They trusted her, saw a lovely woman. And she was, JJ. That's the hell of it. She was a lovely woman who never changed in the eyes of the people here. But she did change in ways no one could see and I never could find a way to make that right. Not for her, not for us. Which is why I'd already separated from her. Because of Max, she scared me, and I didn't trust her. Didn't trust her with our son, either. That's why I have to make it right for Max now. Uprooting him from the only security he knows would be a terrible thing to do because he does need his… home. More now than ever. I don't want him afraid any more."

"Was he afraid of her?"

Dermott nodded. "I think so. He's never said anything, but I think he must have been."

Jenna's heart broke for both of them—for Dermott, for the guilt he felt, and for Max for being afraid of the person he'd trusted to take care of him. She understood how that felt. Fearing her father had been far worse than the feel of his leather belt cracking down on her flesh, or the bone of his knuckle slamming into her cheekbone. Her fear was always the worst part because it never went away. Eventually, the pain did. Until the next time.

"That's why I have to be here for Max, no matter what. I wasn't there for Nancy the way she needed, but I'll always be here for my son."

"But what about your best interests, Dermott? Doesn't that count for anything?"

"No."

He stared straight at her when he said the word, and it was so full of cold, empty sadness it caused a chill to run up her arms. This was the old Dermott, every last bit of him. But now he was marred by time and tragedy. He was there, though, and not buried so deep that she had to look very hard to find him. And when she looked, she knew she wasn't leaving Dermott, or Fort Dyott, for a while. Not unless he sent her away.

Maybe, for a little while, this *could* be home. Dermott made her want it to be.

CHAPTER SEVEN

THEY ate, drank a little more wine, explored the riverbank for rocks, and waded into the water up to their ankles. "It's cold!" Jenna squealed, trying to pull away from Dermott, who had a firm grip on her wrist. The unexpected chill of early fall had already spread its way up her back and she was shivering. But as much from his touch as the cold.

"It's cold because you're a city girl. If you lived out here, it would be invigorating, not cold."

"I'll admit it, I'm city." She tried pulling away again, but his hold only tightened and her shivers only romped up and down even harder. So she tried backing away from him, but he moved forward as she went backwards.

"A city girl who's about to take a plunge into good, hearty Canadian water coming straight down from the mountains. Good thing it's still summer waters, or else they'd be *really* cold."

"No." She laughed nervously. "You wouldn't. Would you?" Again, she tried to break free but this time he pulled her straight into his chest. "You're not going to let me go until you turn me into a shivering ice sculpture, are you?" They'd let go of all the serious topics a while ago, trying not to allow the pall of past tragedies to slip down over their evening, and she was amazed by how much fun she was having with him now, doing something silly like wading in ice-cold water.

"I think you'd be a beautiful ice sculpture," he said, his voice raspy, and not because of the chilly water. "Perfect lines. Perfect design." The look he gave her was very suggestive. "Nice, curvaceous chiseling. A masterwork in ice, or in anything else."

"Ice sculpture isn't in the job description," she said, laughing as the struggle in her started melting into acquiescence. In all honesty, she wasn't that cold, standing this close to him. She was just afraid *not* to be cold because anything else imposed a meaning on her shivers and goose-bumps she just didn't want to be there.

"Then you didn't read the job description. Page six, the fine print at the bottom of the page. The clause that specifically states that the doctor is allowed to have his way with the nurse in the cold, mountain stream, even if that involves ice sculptures."

"Page seven, fine print at the bottom specifically states that the nurse is entitled to fight back any way she can." Except she didn't feel much like fighting back. But this was just too…cozy. Too dangerous. And there was no one to walk through the closet door to stop them once they got started, the way her supervisor had that day. So Jenna feigned a stumble over one of the rocks and in the instant he let go to catch her she made her move. A quick spin in the other direction and she was halfway to the bank before he caught up with her.

"Good move," he said, kicking a little water at her as she dodged him and turned downstream.

"There's more where that came from," she called back over her shoulder, not steady enough to both turn around to see where he was while keeping her footing. She chose steady footing, laughing so hard as she slipped and slid over the smooth river rocks that she wasn't paying much attention to where she was going.

"I think I like your moves," he called back. "They've gotten better over the years. More seductive."

"You think I'm trying to seduce you?" she called back, then paused for a second to hear his response. That's when he grabbed her from behind, then, in the blink of an eye, they were locked in a kiss so hard, so swift, it threatened to rob her of breath. There was so much urgency in the way his mouth claimed hers, in the way his tongue explored places no one else had ever explored. No one but Dermott.

"It's too cold here for this," she finally managed to say. "I think we should…" Before the rest of her words were out, she was in his arms and he was carrying her back to their picnic spot then lowering her to the blanket next to the fire he'd built earlier. And this time there were no barriers. No cold water. No slippery rocks. Only the crackling of the warm fire, and a soft blanket to protect them from the rough pine needles and twigs on the ground. Her perfect fantasy, once-upon-a-time.

He was beautiful, in the orange glow cast off by the firelight. As he stood over her pulling first his jacket over his head, then his shirt, all she could do was stare. It was a body she knew so well, one she'd explored so thoroughly, yet it was new to her again. There was a different hardness in the muscles of his abdomen, his shoulders were broader. And his hips, as his jeans slid down over them, were tighter. "Are you sure?" he asked, as his jeans rode down over the bulge of his erection.

Of many things, no. Of this… "You remembered my birthday, didn't you?"

He grinned. "And if I said yes?"

"Then I'd say yes."

"And if I said no?"

"I'd still say yes."

"Yes," he whispered. "I remembered."

"Yes," she whispered back. "I'm sure."

Three simple words, and Dermott dropped to his knees above her, straddling her. Then he bent to kiss her again, but this time more tenderly. "I remembered so many other things," he said, his voice hoarse with desire. "Didn't want to, but I did."

"So did I. Like, this." She entwined her fingers around his neck and pulled him closer to her, and parted his lips with her tongue to enjoy the taste of him. Pure ambrosia. He'd always tasted of pure ambrosia, and nothing had changed. Their kiss turned urgent again, but this time from her urgency more than his.

"I'm wet," she finally whispered, to which he responded with a moan.

"Not like that, Dermott. My clothes are…soaked."

He pushed off her for a moment, then grinned. "Is that an invitation?"

"More like a demand. I'm freezing."

It didn't take him but two seconds to strip away everything she wore, and it didn't take him but another two seconds to cover her right breast with his hand while his lips sought the nipple on her left. His tongue flicked back and forth as she literally bit down on her lower lip to keep from crying out. Not that anybody out here would have heard her. But she didn't want to cry out yet, didn't want to do anything to cause him to stop what he was doing, even if stopping meant he would move on to something even more pleasurable. She wanted time to stand still at this place and time, so she could enjoy Dermott's every nuance. It had been so long, and she'd had so many fantasies about his lips on her…exploring her, tasting her, giving her so much pleasure…

Still, she couldn't help the moan that did pass through her lips. It escaped as he left her breast and began his journey down…down… "Dermott," she gasped. That was all she had to say. In the next instant, he had nudged in between her legs but… What was he doing? He was moving, but not with her. More like he was struggling against her. "What?" she asked, so aroused even this unusual movement of his naked body on hers felt good.

He chuckled low and deep. "You'll see." And she did. In one swift motion, he rolled her over, twice, and they were literally wrapped in a cocoon inside the blanket—wrapped so tightly together nothing could have come between them.

It was odd…stimulating…feeling him literally bound to her. Feeling the total press of him to her, inch to inch, breath to breath.

"You like?" he asked.

"I like. But how are we going to—?"

Apparently, Dermott knew the answer to her question, as he plunged deep inside her…not in a big, explosive way, but in such an intimate, close way where they never parted, not even for a fraction of a second. It was like nothing she'd ever felt before and she could have stayed there, just like that, forever. Their lovemaking, constrained by the blankets, wasn't fast, neither was it urgent. But it was so intense that when they could no longer hold off their release, Jenna was almost sad. Happy, yet sad. And satisfied in a way she hadn't known possible. Not even with Dermott all those years ago.

Afterwards, in no hurry to go anywhere or do anything, they stayed cocooned in their blanket, exchanging gentle kisses, relishing the feel of spent passion and warm fire and total connection.

"You OK?" he finally asked a little while later. "Warm enough?"

"Fine," she said, almost purring like a kitten.

"Is this something we need to talk about, or act on?"

"You mean like should we have done what we just did?"

"I meant you still naked under that blanket, me still naked under the blanket…"

"Is that why you brought me out here, Dermott? To seduce me?"

"Maybe."

"Well, all I can say is that I've always thought in terms of the perfect seduction as something with silk sheets and champagne. But fleecy cotton and river water certainly have an appeal." This was nice—innocent flirting leading to something much nicer again. And it was leading them right back. They were side-by-side now, still in their blanket, although the cocoon was rather loose, and she tucked her head into his chest and nuzzled closer. "It doesn't always have to be so complicated, does it? I mean, why not enjoy the moment without overthinking it?"

Dermott laughed. "You, not overthink? When has that ever happened?"

"A little while ago, when the blanket was tight and there was nothing but us…" She sighed, then snuggled a little more. "I'll bet you never had anything like this in mind when you came up here as a little boy."

He ducked his head and whispered in her ear. "Want to see what the big boy has on his mind…again?"

"Definitely," she whispered back. "And quickly, before I start to overthink."

"You didn't happen to bring marshmallows to roast over the fire, did you?"

They'd stayed wrapped in that blanket another hour, talking, making love, talking some more. It was only when the chill of the night overtook them that they had to resign themselves to clothes made warm by the fire and jackets and a spot for the blanket much closer to the fire so they could stay warm.

"What's a bonfire without marshmallows?" And seduction. Damn, what had he been thinking? What they'd done… he didn't take it lightly. Right now he wanted, no, he *needed* their working relationship to succeed. What he wanted was something entirely different, something that came with more blankets and marshmallows and moments by the fire. But he couldn't have it, couldn't give it either. Even if he could, Jenna deserved more than what he had here for her. She was like a sparrow on the end of the branch, always on the verge of taking flight. He knew that. Knew that when he'd first met her, knew that over the years when he'd asked various colleagues what they'd heard about Jenna Lawson and they'd told him she'd moved on again.

And here he was, trying to hold onto something that didn't want to be caught. Not that he wanted to catch it so much as he simply wanted that connection between them again. It had been nice then, and so much nicer now. Yet jumping into any kind of a relationship with anyone, especially Jenna, was just plain irresponsible at this point in his life. He knew that as well as he knew he was holding onto a bag of marshmallows, over-thinking. Overthinking, damn it! Overthinking, just like Jenna did.

Still, his heart was telling him that Jenna wasn't a mistake when in every possible way Jenna herself was telling him she was. So would the bigger fool ignore his heart, or would he ignore the clear warnings from the woman he'd lost his heart to all those years ago and, it seemed, never gotten over? "Yep, I've got the marshmallows, and you get to go find the sticks," he said, tossing them at her.

"You think of everything," Jenna said, running off to a nearby thicket to look for a couple of sticks for the toasting.

"That's the problem," he muttered to himself, as he plunked down by the fire. "I think I probably do."

"I, um…I came by to thank the doc for his house call the other night. And you too. I know I should have done this sooner but we've been driving back and forth to Edmonton so much, and with Alisa being upset the way she has been…"

Ron Charney looked uncomfortable standing in the door-way, unsure whether to come all the way in or speak his piece and leave. For a moment, Jenna wondered if his wife had come with him, but when she thought further about it, she knew better.

"We've been calling to check on Joshua, and the reports are excellent. He's doing better than expected." Stiff conversation, but what else was there? "Would you like to speak with Dermott?"

The man shook his head. "I've got to get going. Alisa and I are going back down to the hospital today, and it's a long drive. But I wanted to do the right thing here. And I'm sorry for…" He swallowed hard. "For everything. The doc deserved better."

He did, but it wouldn't do any good to make Ron feel any worse about the situation than he already did. The man looked totally torn up by this. Probably a combination of his wife's re-actions and what might have happened to his son if she'd gotten her way, and his worry over his son. That, coupled with exhaustion from the long drives back and forth caused Jenna to worry about him. He was pale. Looked stressed. "Are you feeling well, Mr. Charney? Would you like Dr. Callahan to have a look at you?"

"I'm a little tired. But it'll get better when we get Joshua home in a few days. Maybe when things settle down I'll stop by for a physical…if you think he'll see me."

"Of course he'll see you! He does understand your wife's feelings, and he won't hold that against you if you need him."

"Feelings that could have killed my son." He shook his head. "Sorry, that's not your problem."

But it was a big one the Charneys would have to face sooner or later, and she felt sorry for them. "Well, to make things easier for your wife, when you get Joshua home, we've made arrangements to have one of the doctors over in Muledeer take over his care. It's still a long drive, but not nearly as long as going to Edmonton, and under the circum-stances we thought it would be in Joshua's best interests to make that change. But in the mean time, if you need anything, we're available here, for any of you. And that includes Joshua's care when he's home, if Alisa changes her mind."

"I appreciate that, ma'am, but I don't think…" Pausing, he shook his head. "With things being the way they are, I don't think Alisa will let the doc near Joshua again, but I do appreciate what you've done. And like I said, I don't have those same feelings so I'll be calling for an appointment soon."

"You do that. Or just stop by whenever you want to. And get some rest, Mr. Charney. You need to take care of yourself."

"One more thing. Joshua would like to see Max. Maybe when my boy's home and settled in, Frank or Irene can bring Max by. If the doc is agreeable."

"I'll mention it to him."

Ron nodded, and smiled. But the smile was forced and painful. "I love my wife, Miss Lawson. She's a good woman and she loves our boy more than you can imagine. But she blames herself, for not seeing… It is what it is with her, and I don't think it's going to change for a long time, if ever."

"I'm sorry for her pain," Jenna replied, then turned and walked back to the exam rooms after Ron had left.

"I'm sorry," Dermott said. He was sitting at his desk, making notes in a patient chart, when she walked by the door.

"You heard?"

"I heard."

"She's wrong, but how can you fight someone who's experiencing so much pain?"

"You can't, which is why Dr. Anderson will look after Joshua. Alisa is entitled to her opinions and forcing the issue in any way just hurts more people…people who don't need the pain," he said.

"Will you let Max go and see Joshua?"

He shrugged, but didn't answer, and Jenna didn't know if that near-refusal, which was what it was, had more to do with Dermott's need to keep Max close, or his fear that Alisa would say something. The thing was, if Alisa had loved Nancy like a sister, she wouldn't hurt Nancy's son. And Dermott did have over-protection issues going on. But decisions regarding Max were none of her business even if, in her opinion, allowing the boys some time together would be good for both of them.

"Well, if you decide to do it, I can make the arrangements, if you want."

"Aren't you going to say something, Jenna? Offer your opinion, tell me what I'm doing wrong? Isn't this where you're suppose to tell me that I'm doing what's best for me and not what's best for Max?"

Well, the wonderful feelings from last night were definitely over, weren't they? They'd lingered by the fire until it had died out, talking, laughing, reminiscing, then returned home, finished that bottle of wine together, and parted company in a nice mellow glow in the wee hours. A lovely evening. She'd enjoyed it more than she'd enjoyed anything since she couldn't remember when. But here they were, back to normal again. It was like the instant they returned to the clinic, the weight of all the problems came crashing back. She felt it, and it showed on Dermott too. "I wasn't going to say anything," she said dispiritedly. "Not a word because it's none of my business. But if you want my opinion—"

"I already know your opinion," he snapped, then his tone changed immediately. "And I respect it, JJ. But I don't know if letting him go is the right thing to do."

"You'll figure it out, Dermott. And you'll do what's right."

"Sometimes it would be nice not doing what's right, but what I really want to do."

"You mean like you and Max running off to somewhere like Costa Rica and never looking back?"

"I'm that transparent?"

"Not really, but that's the way I would think, and I just took a wild guess." She laughed. "I hope I'm not rubbing off on you."

"I hope you are, JJ."

Before she could react, or respond to that, the bell over the door jingled the entrance of another patient, and so it went for the rest of the day. Several patients came in, nothing serious. And another few called to schedule appointments. Then the day ended, and this time there was no invitation to a picnic in the woods, for which she was totally grateful if not a little disappointed. But after they'd closed the clinic she did agree to ride along with Dermott when he went to bring Max home, promising herself that she'd stay in the truck.

Irene invited her in, however, and actually had a plate set at the dinner table for her. Which made her feel ill at ease. This was the house in which Dermott's wife had grown up, and here she was being welcomed into it, almost like she was part of the family. It didn't feel right. "You told me we'd just run out and go back," she whispered to Dermott as Irene carried huge platters of potatoes and corn to the table. "I don't want to have dinner here, Dermott. A peanut butter sandwich at the table outside is one thing, but this is a family situation and I don't feel good about it."

"I didn't know they were going to do this, or I wouldn't have suggested you ride out with me. I know it's uncomfortable for you. Hell, it's not always comfortable for me either."

That surprised her. "Could you make my excuses, and thank them for the invitation?"

"And you'll do what?"

"Walk back. It's not that far. Just a couple of kilometers, and it's a nice evening. I can stop in the diner along the way and have a salad." And try to reconcile herself to the fact that this was the way it was going to be. The only way it could be.

"They have great burgers," he said, the hint of a smile creeping to his lips.

"Then I'll have a burger."

"And french fries. Oh, and you've got to have a chocolate milkshake."

"If I wanted a milkshake, it would be vanilla. Or strawberry."

He shook his head. "Has to be chocolate. That's the only thing that goes with a burger and fries, unless you'd prefer a root beer."

"Actually, I love root beer."

"Then it's a date." He looked over at the table, at Max settling into his usual spot there, and sighed heavily. "Look, folks, I appreciate the offer of dinner, but I told you earlier not to fix anything for us, that Max and I had other plans."

Irene looked up, a frown crossing her face. "But you always say that, dear. Then you sit down and have dinner with us anyway."

"Because I have a pathetically boring life," he said under his breath.

Jenna laughed, then whispered, "Let's see how you're going to get yourself out of this one. She's fixed enough food for an army and there's no gracious way for you to walk away from it." Even though that's what she still intended on doing.

"And I need an army right now." He sucked in a deep breath and headed back to the table, but Jenna followed him only to the dining room doorway, then stopped.

"I appreciate your generosity," she said to Irene and Frank, "but I really did have other plans for the evening, and I can't stay."

"You're not comfortable with us," Irene said.

"Not entirely. I don't do well in family situations." That much was true, she didn't. "And, I, um…I really think it's best if I go."

"You are welcome here," Irene said, a warm, sincere smile wrinkling her face, "but I do understand. I'm not entirely comfortable with Frank's family, and they're actually family." She teased her husband with a wink. "But, please, know that you're welcome here anytime."

After saying her goodbyes, Jenna was all the way down the front walk and halfway across the street when Dermott caught up with her. "Damn," he said, falling into step. "You sure do move fast."

"What are you doing?" she muttered. "You should have stayed."

"And Irene and Frank thought I should go, so they kicked me out."

"They didn't kick you out."

"OK, they strongly suggested that I come after you."

"No, they didn't."

"Yes, they did. They didn't think you should be alone, and they felt bad for creating a situation that made you uncomfortable, so…" He shrugged.

She stopped to face him. "But you didn't have to do this for me, Dermott. I'm fine by myself."

"I did it for me, JJ. I mean, they're good people but sometimes I have to cut myself loose from them." He shook his head. "That probably doesn't make any sense, does it?"

"It makes a lot of sense, actually. And I think you're better than almost anybody I've ever known in the way you deal with an awkward situation. What I do when it isn't comfortable for me is walk away, and I admire that you've stuck it out."

"Because they didn't do anything, and don't deserve to be hurt. So, how about we go back and get the truck?"

"Then?"

"We could play the truck driver and the hitchhiker?" he asked, giving his eyebrows a wicked wiggle.

She liked him when he was incorrigible. Maybe that's when she liked him best. "Only if the truck driver takes the hitchhiker to the diner for a burger, because this hitchhiker is starved."

"I had another scenario in mind," he teased, feigning disappointment.

"Is it the one where the hitchhiker turns down the truck driver's offer of a ride and walks to the diner alone?"

"You're no fun, JJ," he moaned, turning around and heading back for the truck.

"I might be if I can have some french fries with that burger," she called after him. "And a *vanilla* milkshake."

* * *

The diner was lively when they walked in. Lots of people crammed into the booths and around the tables, lots of chatter, lots of laughter. They stood outside at the door for a minute, just looking in.

"Chocolate milkshake," he warned. "That's the only true way to do it."

"Then I'm not sure I want to be seen with you, Doctor, because you seem to have a particularly closed mind, and I like to think of myself as an open-minded kind of a girl."

"Guilt by association, Nurse Lawson. You've already been seen with me." He pointed to the several faces smiling at them. "The secret's out."

She laughed. "Will it shock their sensibilities when they see you out with someone other than Max?"

"Probably. About half the people in there have nominated me to sainthood, which I believe dooms me to a celibate life, or something like it."

"I think they'd take back that nomination if they'd seen you wrapped up in that blanket with me. Nothing celibate going on there."

"Not fair reminding me in a place where I can't do anything about it."

"About what?"

"I believe the correct medical terminology is—"

Jenna pinched his arm to shut him up. "Not here," she hissed. "Someone might hear you, then…"

"Then what?"

"Then they'd know what we did." She glanced around to make sure no one was eavesdropping.

"People do it, Jenna. Surely, that was one of the lessons they taught you in nursing school. You know, it's one of those natural acts, been going on for years now."

"Very funny," she whispered, trying to fight the blush threatening to overtake her. How was it that everything with

Dermott turned into something so sexy, like this had all of a sudden? "You know what I'm talking about."

"I believe it started with a burger and fries." He bent down to whisper in her ear. "And an erection."

This time she slapped him on the arm, and walked on ahead of him as the waitress led her to a booth near the rear.

Heads turned, of course, as Dermott followed on behind. And about half the people quit talking as Dermott and Jenna walked by them. But amazingly, after the first rush of gawks and whispers were over, things returned to normal and by the time they were seated, people weren't paying much attention to them at all.

"It's like a martyr walking to his doom," Dermott muttered, as he took his seat across from her.

"In your imagination. So, why didn't Max come?"

"Grandma's chocolate cake has a lot of persuasive power. And I did ask him if he wanted to come with us."

"Grandma's chocolate cake…" Jenna licked her lips, then sighed. "I don't blame him. My grandmother made the most wonderful buttermilk cake." Fond memories of better days. She hadn't thought of one of her grandmother's cakes in years, and now she craved it.

"What kind of icing?"

"White."

"You mean vanilla. As in a vanilla milkshake?"

"Because vanilla's best." Her grandmother's vanilla icing had been, anyway. "If you're not too set in your chocolate ways to give it a try."

"Chocolate," he said. One word, and one word only in that argument.

The diner was a cozy place, and it was nice that the people working there were beginning to recognize her as a regular customer. She'd never been a regular anything to anybody before, and this recognition, as slight as it was, did give her a sense of belonging. Just a little. "I've had at least one meal a day here since I've arrived," she said, "and I've never ordered a chocolate anything."

"Then you don't know what you're missing."

"Or maybe I do! Which is why I prefer vanilla."

"There's nothing easy about you, JJ. I knew that back then, and I know it more than ever now. You're stubborn for the sake of being stubborn."

"Because we disagree on which flavor is best?" This was fun. Dermott was fun. Sometimes it was nice being silly over nothing—just putting the important things aside for a while and existing in the moment. She didn't do that so often…hardly ever…no, *never*. But she was enjoying it now, like she had on the riverbank, especially since she was doing it with Dermott.

"We wouldn't disagree if you'd admit I'm right."

"Can I help you?" the waitress asked.

"I'd like a burger with everything on it, fries and a chocolate milkshake," Dermott said, snapping shut his menu and handing it back to the waitress.

"Same for me, except make my milkshake vanilla."

"The lady would also like a chocolate milkshake," Dermott added, keeping a straight face.

"And the gentleman would also like a vanilla milkshake," Jenna added, her face also straight.

"Two milkshakes each?" the waitress asked, without so much as a lift of a speculative eyebrow.

"For a total of four," Jenna confirmed.

Dermott let out a low whistle as the waitress walked away. "You are stubborn, JJ. In fact, I think you've perfected it to an art form."

"Does that threaten you?"

A slow, sexy grin spread across his face as he relaxed back into the booth. "I wouldn't define it as threatening. I'd say it's more like admiration. A woman who would actually go through with ordering two milkshakes for herself just to prove her point has my attention and my admiration. That is, if she drinks both those milkshakes."

"You think I won't? Or I can't?"

"You know what, JJ? I think you can do anything you put your mind to."

It was nice having someone express that kind of confidence in her, even if it was only over a milkshake or two. The only problem was, she didn't have that same confidence. Not in her life. Not in her desires. Not even in her ability to drink two milkshakes. And it always got back to that, even in the nice moments like these. "I think I'm going to go find that waitress," she said, scooting to the edge of the booth, "and change my order."

Dermott leaned across the table and grabbed her wrist before she stood. "It starts with the big leaps, Jenna. One milkshake is a baby step, two turns it into a big leap."

"What are you talking about?"

"Trusting yourself. Believing that you can do what you set out to do, have what you set out to have. Taking the leap that's big enough to make a difference in some way. And it doesn't matter what kind of leap it is so long as you can prove to yourself that you can do it."

"You're assuming I want to leap," she snapped.

He let go of her wrist, but didn't say another word. Instead, he folded his arms across his chest and simply stared at Jenna. It was a stare that went right through her, made her feel naked and vulnerable, because it was a stare that told her he knew her so well. In ways, better than she knew herself.

So, the next step was up to her. She could cancel the second milkshake, which was the same old predictable Jenna Lawson, or she could go for it. All the way. "OK, so maybe you're right about me and my baby steps," she admitted, sliding back into the booth. "But do you really think I'm going to be able to move, let alone leap, after I drink two milkshakes?"

"You've already leaped," he said, reaching across the table and taking hold of her hand.

She had, hadn't she? One big leap in such a small, insignificant thing. She felt good. Probably much better than she would feel at the end of the meal, she thought as the waitress plonked two huge milkshakes down in front of her. "Better to leap now than after I drink these," she said, pulling the chocolate one over to her.

The burgers were perfect, but Dermott hardly noticed because Jenna had his undivided attention. She didn't have to do anything other than dip her french fry in ketchup to capture him, and he was definitely captured. Body, soul…heart. Totally in love. Oh, he'd been toying with it all along. Admitting it, taking it back, admitting it again, taking it back again. Now, though, there was no more taking it back, and that made his problem even bigger. Protecting Max, trying to hide all the ugly truths from Nancy's parents, and trying to find out how Jenna fit into all this…it was an insane juggling act, and he hated being a juggler. What he wanted was stability. A calm life.

But he loved Jenna and, in some absurd way, he was pretty sure she loved him too. Or else why would she have stayed here, in the middle of all this uncertainty? For sure, she could have a better professional life just about anywhere. And she really didn't have any kind of a social life. So something was holding her and he hoped it was her feelings for him, and even for Max. Or maybe he was being sloppy and sentimental over something that simply wasn't there. Jenna landed, stayed a while, then flew away, and maybe that was in her ticket for what she had in mind to do here.

Damn that uncertainty creeping in again.

Still, he'd loved her at first sight the first time. The hell of it was, he'd loved her at first sight the second time too, that day in the elevator. Even when he'd known better. But no matter how bad it got, Jenna made it better, made it seem like all his other problems weren't beating him down. So what was wrong with living in the moment…living in Jenna's moment? "Want to know when I first knew that we were going to get involved?" he asked, trying to push aside his doubts and live in *this* moment.

She shoved aside both milkshakes. "We were putting a halo on that patient with a broken neck."

He shook his head. "It was that day you stood up to Dr. McNichol."

"I was a registered nurse, and he wanted me to fetch him coffee. I had ten patients to see, charts to take care of, phone calls to make, doctors' orders to fulfill, and the man wanted me to stop in the middle of everything, drop what I was doing and go get him a cup of coffee. What was I supposed to have done?"

"He was the chief of service. Most people would have done what he asked."

"And I was a floor nurse who was doing the work of three. Fetching coffee wasn't what I got two college degrees to do, it wasn't in my job description, and he didn't have the right to make that request of me, not when he was capable of walking across the hall to the lounge and getting his own coffee. And I filed a complaint over it when he yelled at me, in case you never heard about that."

"He yelled at you because you marched over to the lounge and brought him the whole pot of coffee. It was an industrial-sized pot, Jenna. Held fifty cups."

She laughed. "He got his coffee, didn't he? And he never asked me for anything outside the job I was paid to do again. No one else did, either."

"That was the first time I ever saw you, and you were breathing fire, carrying that big coffeemaker down the hall, its cord dragging behind. People were running to get out of your way." Sexy as hell, determined. He'd known then she was a woman to be reckoned with. Fierce to the bone in defense of something or someone she believed in. That hadn't changed. She still was, and he wondered what it would have been like for Max to have a mother who so ferociously defended him rather than... No! He wasn't going to think about that now. He had the dark hours to deal with the bitter recoil of those feelings. Now was for pleasant thoughts.

"Do you think that's the reason they transferred me to another department the next week?"

"As I recall, you were transferred a few times in the next few weeks." Her eyes fairly sparked with mischief now, and he loved that. Hadn't seen it so much since she'd come to live in Fort Dyott and that was a pity.

"I was young and foolish."

"Never foolish, Jenna." He paused while the waitress cleared away their plates, then scampered away. "You always had some kind of a purpose or mission, and you let people know what it was, but it was never foolish."

"All I ever wanted to do was give good patient care. People always got in the way of that, paperwork became more important than the patients. Hospital policies impinged on common-sense procedure. It got to be a maze, Dermott. One you couldn't find your way through, and I got frustrated." She smiled. "More than once. And with frustration came my transfers, then job changes, because I couldn't hold my tongue, or I wouldn't do the paperwork when the patient needed real care. I don't suppose I was meant to fit into the system." She laughed. "Or maybe I was meant to devise the system. I don't know. But however it was, I did sort of have this pattern of behavior, didn't I?" She signaled for the waitress to take away the milkshakes. She'd tried both, had had as much as she could manage. "I still have it, and I guess it's probably not going to change. Like my preference for vanilla."

Which was what scared him. Jenna was Jenna, and expecting her to be anything else was tantamount to a crime. He'd learned that years ago, and had thought about it so much since she'd come here. Jenna, being Jenna, was what he liked. Even with all her complications.

"Well, some of your patterns are very nice," he admitted, shoving away his vanilla milkshake. "But you're right. Some things probably won't change." No matter how much he wanted them to. And he did want them to.

CHAPTER EIGHT

HER phone was ringing. Or was that the doorbell downstairs?

Jenna turned over in bed and squinted at the clock. Three-fifteen! She'd been sleeping like a baby for hours, pleasant dreams of ice-cream parlors and handsome boyfriends, and the shrill of the phone snapped her out of it as surely as a pail of ice cold water on her face would have. She bolted up in bed and lunged for her phone. "Hello," she gasped into the receiver.

"Miss Lawson, this is Alisa Charney." The voice on the other end was frail, wobbly. Crying. "It's my husband. He's awfully sick...needs help. I can't get him out of bed."

"Symptoms?" Jenna asked, scooting to the edge of the bed, getting ready to toss on the first clothes she could find.

"Short of breath, chest pains... Maybe he's sick to his stomach. I can't tell for sure."

All kinds of things went through her mind, none of them good. "We'll be there in twenty minutes," Jenna said. "*Dr. Callahan* and myself. In the meantime, try to get your husband to sit up a little, or at least recline back on his pillows so he's not lying flat. And keep an eye on his breathing."

"Please, hurry," the woman cried, not even protesting that Dermott was going to be making this house call, too. That meant Ron had to be awfully sick. Or dying.

"I couldn't get a good sense of the symptoms," she explained to Dermott, who had answered his door still groggy, and looking so sexy in his low-riding pajama bottoms and mussed hair. "But it could be a heart attack, maybe acid indigestion…"

He turned away from the door and ran to dress while she went to Max's room to rouse him from sleep. Beautiful little boy, she thought as she scooped him up in her arms. He looked like Dermott, only with blond hair.

"We going for a ride?" Max asked, barely opening his eyes at her.

"Your daddy has to go see somebody who's sick, and—"

"No!" he cried, squirming out of her arms. He hit the floor with a thud, then curled up right where he fell, on the oval crocheted throw rug, and went right back to sleep.

"What's going on?" Dermott called from the other room.

"Max doesn't want to get out of bed." And she couldn't blame him.

Dermott stepped into the doorway and took a look. "Can you stay here with him while I go? I don't like disturbing him all the time."

"I can, but that means you'll have to go face Alisa alone." She bent down, picked up the little boy and laid him back in his bed. "Are you sure you want to do that?"

"What I'm sure of is that I don't want to disturb my son in the middle of the night. If Alisa can't deal with that she can call someone over in Muledeer."

Jenna knew he wouldn't make the woman do that, but she liked hearing Dermott say it. Of course, come morning, Alisa would have a new round of gripes about Dermott, but it warmed her heart that Dermott didn't pay any attention to the inevitable as he trudged out in the middle of the night. He was a good man, and the more she watched him, the more she understood how good. In the end, that's what mattered the most, she decided as she lay down in his bed, pulled up his sheets and drifted off, smelling the scent of him all around her.

* * *

The alarm was sounding, and she didn't want to get up, but the sun was streaming in through the blinds, trying to force her eyes open. Which she resisted.

She did turn over to swat the alarm, only to be obstructed by something she didn't expect. It was Max, curled into her side. Lying there, sucking his thumb, a picture of innocence, he looked like a perfect angel. Yes, he had come in looking for Dermott a little while after his father had gone. She remembered that. He hadn't been having a scary dream, as he called it, but he was afraid he might, so she'd let him crawl in with her, like that was the natural thing to do.

And she'd slept very well. Having this child in her arms...it was a feeling she couldn't describe, didn't understand. But she liked it. Liked it more than she wanted to. "You ready to get up?" she asked him.

In answer, he bounded off the bed and ran across the room, heading straight for the bedroom door, then the hall, then his own bedroom.

Laughing, Jenna scooted to the edge of the bed wishing she had that same kind of energy in the morning, wishing she didn't have to leave Dermott's bed, wishing Dermott was right there with her.

Had he come home yet? She didn't know, but she was curious, so she trudged out to the living room where Dermott was sprawled out on the couch, sound asleep. He looked like Max when he slept, in the way his hair was mussed, the way he was twisted slightly to his side. Looking almost innocent.

She stood and studied him for a moment, then decided to go back to her apartment. It was still too early for work, but she could grab a quick shower, go outside for a walk and have enough time to stop by the diner for a light breakfast. Her departure from the apartment was stopped, though, when Dermott rolled over and opened his eyes. "Indigestion," he said, his voice rough and sexy from sleep.

"You're referring to Ron and not yourself, aren't you?"

Sitting up, Dermott brushed the hair back from his eyes and indulged in a good, long stretch. His clothes were crumpled, dark stubble on his face emphasized that he hadn't shaved in twenty-four hours, and his blue eyes were heavy from lack of sleep, all of it making Dermott Callahan just about the sexiest man she'd ever seen in her life. The unkempt look suited him and, to be honest, she liked it better that the polished perfection she'd come to know in the hospital. That had been all for show and image, and she understood that. But this was the essential Dermott, and he was a breath-taker, to be sure.

"Ron has acid reflux, severe case of it. He's under a lot of stress and it all backed up on him. I gave him a prescription, told him the over-the-counter drugs weren't strong enough to do the job, and told him I'd like to send him for some tests. And—"

"Let me guess, " Jenna interrupted. "When Alisa found out he wasn't going to die, your services were no longer needed."

"Something like that. Alisa kept herself at a distance until I determined the problem, then she disappeared altogether after that. Of course, Ron wasn't very easy having me there and there's no good way to tell a man that I suspect his wife is causing him a lot of his problems." He smiled. "Ron knows it, though. You could tell by that agonized look on his face when Alisa's around where the biggest source of his stress is coming from, and I have a hunch that the incident with Joshua didn't help their situation."

"Well, he's lucky his stress didn't cause him a real heart attack. I hope he takes your advice, or goes to another doctor Alisa will approve of."

"I told him he might not be so lucky next time, that he really should have the tests done right away, but Alisa insisted they'd go to Muledeer in a few days and let the doctors there handle everything. So I did everything I could and left. The rest will be up to them." He stood, stretched his long frame, a gesture she couldn't help but admire on a body like his, then plodded to the kitchen and poured himself a glass of water. "By the way, I wanted to crawl into bed with you when I got back but you had another man there with you. It was awfully cozy."

She laughed. "It was, wasn't it?"

"Was it his idea?"

"He was afraid he might have a scary dream."

"Would that work for me? Suppose I told you I might have a scary dream. Would you let me sleep with you?"

"If that spot's not already taken, I might."

"Seriously, is he OK? Because it's not like him to want to sleep with someone…not even me. He's pretty independent that way."

"Well, I was a little worried, but I watched him for a while, and he dozed right off when he crawled into bed. And he has lots of energy this morning, so that'll prove he had a pretty good night."

"Better night than I had," he commented.

Jenna pulled in a tormented breath, weighing her words before she spoke, as what she had to say was so dreadful. So painful. But she couldn't hold back, couldn't keep it to herself because she'd seen what she'd seen, and it was Dermott's right to know. So, finally, she said it. "He flinched, Dermott. When I went to fix the pillow under his head, and reached across him, he flinched."

A flash of comprehension flickered in Dermott's eyes, but he didn't let on. "And…"

"Hands up over his face, a defensive posture. Only for a moment. Then he was fine."

Dermott nodded, swallowing hard. "This is something Frank and Irene are never to know. Do you understand that, Jenna? I don't want them finding out."

Her stomach knotted. *She already knew what he was going to tell her.* She'd recognized it when Max had flinched and pulled up to protect himself, because that's what she used to do. Still did sometimes, when she was caught off guard. "She abused him," she whispered, so Max wouldn't overhear. "His mother abused him."

Agony spread across Dermott's face. "I found out, too late, that she would lock him in his room, then live the life she wanted to that day. Leave the house, take her drugs, see her various men. She'd get home before I did, and let him out. Sometimes she'd just lock him in the house and let him have the run of it when she went out."

"Did Max tell you?"

"No, he never said a word."

Like she hadn't said a word, even when people who'd suspected had asked.

"I had a bad headache one morning. A migraine. I didn't want to work through it because my patients needed better from me, so I had my nurse cancel my appointments, and I went home to go to bed just shortly after noon. Nancy wasn't there, but Max was, all alone. Apparently she hadn't fed him and he'd climbed up on a chair to get to a box of dry cereal. He'd…" He shut his eyes and bit his lip. "He'd poured it on the floor and eaten it off the floor. And he was so scared, Jenna." Dermott's voiced trailed off into almost nothing. "My little boy was so scared. I'll never forget the look on his face when I walked in. If I live to be a hundred, I'll never forget…"

"Oh, my God," she gasped. "I'm so sorry." The stark pain in his eyes hurt her heart.

"So was I, especially when I learned that she'd done this other times. Many times. She'd lock him in for the day then go do what she wanted to."

The way her father had locked her up, then left her. "Did she ever hurt him?" Jenna asked, although she already knew.

"She claimed she didn't, but Max always had bruises. Nancy would say he fell down, or bumped into something. And maybe he did because he was always alone. She insisted that he was a clumsy little boy, and there was nothing to prove otherwise. But he's no more clumsy than any other boys his age and after I took him and left her, I never saw as many bruises on him as I did when she took care of him. So, yes, I think there's a good chance she hit him."

"But her parents don't know?"

"They knew about the drugs…that couldn't be kept quiet after her wreck. And maybe they knew that she was drinking, and seeing other men. But if they'd known she was endangering Max…" He shook his head. "They wouldn't have allowed it. Not even from their daughter. And whatever else they knew, or didn't know, I don't talk about it with them, so I don't know."

"You protect them, though."

"They were good parents, and they're the best grandparents a little boy could ever have. They do right by Max in the ways that matter, and I love them for that. So, yes, I protect them."

"You're a good man, Dermott. I think if people knew…"

"But they won't, because that would hurt my son. People here already feel bad enough with what they know. It's like the whole town absorbed some of the guilt for not seeing it."

"Because she hid it from everybody, not just you. But keep in mind, Dermott, that there was a time you did love her, and as much as you hate everything she did, you need to hang onto some of the good for Max's sake, because he'll need that someday."

"Like he'll need to know how I didn't see what was happening to her? How's he going to react to that, Jenna? His mother was destroying herself by degrees and his father didn't even see it."

"I know you want to blame yourself for what happened, but all you did was what you were supposed to do. And, sure, maybe you were too busy working, maybe you didn't pay enough attention, maybe your marriage was failing for any number of reasons. But we all have blind spots, Dermott.

That's human nature, and you shouldn't beat yourself up for it, because sometimes it's good."

"Good? How can that be good?"

"You fall in love with someone who's not quite perfect, but you don't see the imperfections because you're so much in love. That's a good blind spot."

"Well, I'll concede that point, but that doesn't make me any less responsible for what happened."

"With an addiction, no one is responsible except the one who is addicted. You didn't cause Nancy to become an addict, the way I didn't cause my father to become an alcoholic. There's always a lot of blame to go around but an addiction is a very lonely illness. I spent years and years blaming myself for my dad's addiction because he blamed me for my mother's death, said she was never healthy after she had me, and that her death was my fault. But it wasn't. When I was older, I found her death certificate. She died of virulent pneumonia. I was too young to know if she'd seen a doctor, but I think she probably didn't. With my father's temper, I doubt he would have allowed that. So after she died, he blamed me, and I believed him because, I suppose, in some way I did feel guilty. It's an easy thing to take on yourself, especially when you're so young, and when there are no clear answers why it happened, like with Nancy, or my mother. And people need those answers, Dermott. It's their resolution."

"I'm so sorry, JJ. I'm so caught up in my own mess and just look what you went through yourself."

"My mess is all in the past. Your mess involves a little boy who has some serious things to face in his future." She wouldn't turn this into something about her because it was about Max. And it was about helping Dermott. "Does he ever talk about it?"

Dermott shook his head. "Not a word. But he has those nightmares. The child therapist I took him to down in Edmonton said he'll have memories, but right now they're repressed except in the nightmares, and at some time in the future when they surface they may cause problems. It's just a waiting game."

She knew the waiting game. Knew it well. But for Max, there was someone there to hold him as he waited. He was a lucky little boy.

"It's purple!" Not just purple walls. Purple everywhere. Ceiling, floor, walls. Jenna squinted at what looked like an explosion of grape jelly. "Very, very purple."

"And I'm not!" Max exclaimed, proud of his handiwork.

"Purple's not bad for a bathroom," Dermott conceded. They'd worked all morning, painted everything that could be painted in a bathroom and now his budding Picasso was ready for a nap in spite of that fact that he had purple streaks in his hair. It had been a good morning and, surprisingly for his age, Max hadn't lost interest. The kid had an attention span better than some adults Dermott knew and he was proud of that. "And speaking of purple, I think it's time to take your purple-haired self off to bed for a while, don't you, Max?"

He shook his head to protest, then had second thoughts. 'Just a little one. And when we get up we're going to paint your bathroom."

"Purple?" Jenna asked, as Max scooted down the hall.

"Not if I can hide the purple paint first." Dermott dropped down on the couch and propped his feet up on the table across from it, then patted the seat next to him. "Might as well relax. We've got about an hour before Clyde Fister comes in for a consultation."

"I didn't see it on the books."

"Because he's nervous. Afraid that I'll leave the appointment book open and someone will accidentally see that he's coming in." He settled down into the couch a little more.

"And you're going to keep me in suspense?"

"Thought you might like to guess." He raised a teasing eyebrow.

"I'm playing a game where I have to guess the patient's condition?" Dermott would never disrespect a patient, so this wasn't going to be a patient with a problem.

"He's not exactly the patient."

Now she was curious. "Do we have to unlock the back door for him? Maybe put a trench coat and dark glasses out in the alley for him to wear so no one will recognize him? Check to make sure that Mr. Ketterman isn't out there with his cigar when Mr. Fister comes sneaking in?" This was such a different kind of medicine from anything she'd ever done, and she liked it. Liked knowing the intimate details of her patients... Mr. Ketterman and his once-a-week cigar. Mr. Fister and the secret that was about to be revealed. It made her feel like she belonged somewhere...belonged here. *Right here.*

She did want to believe that, and part of her was letting the feeling seep in and linger. But the other part was spitting it back out because she knew better. She'd had an entire lifetime of knowing better and even though she desperately wanted this situation with Dermott to be different, it wouldn't be. Because, in the end, she was still Jenna Joann Lawson, and nothing about that had changed.

"It's not quite that secret, but it is a big surprise. A birthday gift for his wife." He grinned. "An unusual birthday gift." Pulling a pamphlet from his pocket, he dropped it into Jenna's lap. It was entitled "Hair Plugs".

Jenna blinked. "So let me get this straight. The big secret is that his wife is going to get hair plugs for her birthday?"

Dermott laughed. "Not Mrs. Fister. Mr. Fister. He's been saving his money, stashing it away in secret to do this, and I've helped him find a reputable clinic. Plastic surgeon."

"For his wife. Do you know if his wife really cares?" Jenna glanced up at Dermott's dark brown hair, his angular face, his beautiful blue eyes. All very classically handsome, all very sexy. How would he look without hair?

She shut her eyes for a moment, trying to raise the picture, but all she could get was sexy. And it wasn't in the way he looked so much as the way he was. With or without hair, Dermott was a sexy man and if his looks changed, that wouldn't make him any less sexy to her.

"I think it's more about Mr. Fister's perception of himself than anything. His hair is thin, and he wants it back."

"We all want things back, Dermott, but that doesn't mean we can get them. Or even should get them."

"But what do you do when you're Clyde Fister, who doesn't like what he sees when he looks in the mirror, and there's a way to change that?"

"It shouldn't be about changing what he sees in the mirror. It's more about what you can't see in the mirror." Impulsively, she reached up and ran her fingers through Dermott's hair. "It's a beautiful mane you have, Dr. Callahan, but it doesn't make you who you are."

He shivered under her touch. "Maybe it depends on the person who's there to help you be everything you're supposed to be."

"Then you think it takes two people to help one of them realize their fullest potential, that one person can't do that on their own?"

"Are you trying to provoke something?" he asked, his eyes twinkling.

Scooting closer to Dermott, until they were pressed lightly side-by-side, she leaned her head over on his shoulder. "Sometimes I think I want to. But then other times… It's complicated."

Resisting the natural urge to pull her even closer, Dermott merely took Jenna's hand in hers. It was a quiet, affectionate thing to do that seemed right at that moment. "Well, what I think is that any one person can achieve amazing things on their own. To come into your own doesn't *require* another person, but to have someone there for you, to support you, to sit and hold your hand is much nicer than doing it alone."

"Even if he's five?" she asked.

"Even if she's thirty. We all need someone, JJ. It's easier that way."

"Not always."

"What did your father do to you that keeps you running? What did he do that hurt you so badly you're afraid to let anyone get close?" He could feel her body stiffen, and he fully expected her to get up and leave. So he held on to her hand a little tighter. Enough to let her know that she was supported, but not enough that she felt restrained.

"Drank. Went to work sober, came home and got drunk. Told me I was worthless, that I'd ruined his life."

"You believed that?" There was more. Something she wasn't telling him because she was still rigid, and this seemed so rehearsed. It was the little speech you practiced over and over in your mind for the day when you'd finally have to give it. No emotion. Just words. And if there was one thing he knew about Jenna, she was tied up in so many different layers of emotion, layers all waiting to be peeled back and revealed. It was something he loved most about her because her emotional depths made her so vital, so caring.

"As a little girl, sure I did. You're supposed to believe your parents. Even when they're like my dad was."

"And how was he, Jenna? Other than mean, how was he really?"

She shivered, then shook her head rather than speaking. But she didn't try pulling away from him, which he found surprising. Maybe this little bird didn't want to fly away as badly as he thought she did. Or as *she* thought she did. "How did your father hurt you?"

"He hit me," she said, her voice surprisingly steady. "Every day. It became part of my daily routine. He didn't like the way I fixed his coffee, so he'd hit me. His shirts weren't pressed to suit him so he'd hit me. I was there so he'd hit me."

His stomach started to knot, and he could feel the acid burn of it all the way down. To hit a child like Max, or to hit Jenna...

"Sometimes he'd lock me in the closet. If he didn't want to be bothered with me, he'd shove me in and lock the door."

"For how long?"

"A few hours, maybe. Then he'd let me out." She took in a deep, wobbly breath. "A couple of times he got drunk and forgot and I was in there for a day. But I always knew that he'd come back for me when he needed something."

Dear God, he couldn't even imagine. Not for Jenna, not for Max. "Did he molest you, Jenna?" he asked, trying to sound more like a doctor than the man who loved this woman. But he was the man who loved her and his voice trembled.

"No. I guess even my father drew the line somewhere. And the thing is, I was always glad when he hit me because I knew he wouldn't do it again for a while, then I would have a few hours where I didn't have to be so scared." Finally, a single tear slid down her cheek, and she let it fall. "And I functioned. I went to school when I was supposed to, did my homework, and to everybody looking on, we were a good family. Admirable single dad raising his daughter alone. Pretty little girl making good grades in school, always wearing nice clothes, always smiling. Who would have guessed all the ugly secrets behind our doors?"

No one in town, Dermott thought. Not one single person. Suddenly, he understood. Now that this wasn't about him, he did see it. "But you went to live with your grandparents, didn't you? They saw what was happening?"

"Not until I was thirteen. They'd come to visit unannounced, and literally walked in on us. My father had just slammed me into the wall, and at the point my grandfather walked through the door, my father had hit me only once. He was ready to hit me again. Grandpa asked me how often that happened, and I told him it happened all the time. He took me by the arm, took me out of there, and I never saw my father again."

"Your mother's father?"

Jenna shook her head. "My father's father. My grandfather told me years later that my father had always had a bad temper. That even when he was a little boy my grandparents couldn't control him. But they were sure he'd grow out of it, and they'd never thought he could do anything like he'd done to me. At the time I wanted to believe that, but sometimes I wondered if, deep down, they did know and just couldn't face it. I mean, how do you look at someone you love and see so much ugliness?" She laughed bitterly. "Maybe you don't. Maybe when you love someone that much blind spot keeps growing until it blocks out everything you truly aren't able to deal with. You know, love is blind, and all that."

This was incredible. With the exception of a few details, it was Max's story and, dear God, that scared him in so many ways. He wanted to hold her tighter, wanted to know more, wanted to say so many things, but the doorbell jingled downstairs, and Clyde Fister had arrived to discuss hair plugs. If ever there was a time Dermott didn't want to discuss hair plugs, this was it. But the moment was over. Jenna was pushing away from him now, looking much more composed about what she'd told him than he felt. It was his knees that were wobbling when he stood up, his hands that were shaking, his head that was spinning.

And it was Jenna who walked solidly down the stairs and greeted their patient.

Dermott sagged against the wall at the top of the stairs before he went down, trying to compose himself, trying to make some sense of this. But there was no sense to be found, no composure to be had. He was mad as hell at the bastard who'd hurt Jenna so deeply. Mad as hell at Nancy for what she'd done to Max. Mad at himself. Mad at the world. So mad that he balled his fist and hit the wall. Over and over. Until his fist was bloody and swollen. And that didn't make him feel any better. Not any better about anything.

CHAPTER NINE

JENNA dropped the gauze pad in the trash and pulled a fresh one from the stack. "I don't think anything is broken," she said as she dabbed at the scrapes across his knuckles. "Without X-rays it's hard to tell, but your function is intact, so unless you have complications, like smashing the wall with your other hand, I'd say you'll be better in a day or two. Just keep your hand away from plaster for a while."

"You're not very sympathetic," Dermott grumbled.

"And you're not a very convincing liar."

"I stumbled," he grunted.

"And caught yourself on the wall with your knuckles."

"It's not a big deal."

But it was. She knew why he'd punched the wall. Some of it was for her, some of it was what he saw for Max. She knew that same anger, but she'd had years to put it in its proper place. Dermott was only just now beginning to deal with it. The trouble was, as the outsider looking in, he was experiencing the rage, but not the deep-down kind of emotions that caused people to do the crazy things like run away from a good thing the way she'd done before and would probably do again. Rage resulted in scraped knuckles. The deep-down emotions that tended to keep themselves locked away resulted in scraped lives. "What's a big deal, Dermott, is that someday, somewhere, Max is going to say something to you about what happened to him, and you're going to feel like putting that fist through the wall again. You're justified in your feelings, but Max will need more than your gut reaction, and if he was hit by his mother, that gut action could frighten him. Or, worse, cause him to retreat."

"And you don't think I haven't thought about that? I mean, what if he'd seen me do this?" He held up his battered fist.

She smiled gently. "He didn't. No harm done."

"Isn't there?"

They were in exam one, he on the table, she standing in front of him. Mr. Fister had come and gone, taken his hair-plug pamphlet with him, and promised to try shaving himself totally bald and living with that manly look for a while before he put himself through the new hair ordeal. Jenna had convinced him that a nice head such as his deserved to be on display, and she reminded him how many people were doing that these days. The truth was, he had a look that would support being bald. Maybe an earring, too. But he'd said he'd have to think on that one for a while. "I probably shouldn't have said anything to you. Don't know why I did, because I never talk about it to anyone. Not even my therapist when I was a teenager and my grandparents forced me to have counseling." She'd told him because she'd never known anyone as easy to talk to as Dermott.

"I'm sorry, Jenna. For what you went through. For overreacting. All the time when you were telling me about your father, I was picturing Max with his mother."

"I know," she whispered, as she applied a bandage to his hand, crossing the gauze over the back of his hand and bringing it around to cover his palm. He had nice skin, soft. And nice fingers. She loved those fingers, loved the feel of them on her flesh—just a few nights ago in the stream, just a few years ago... Time blurred for a moment, thinking about the way her skin prickled with the sensation of his touch— prickled even though she didn't want it to.

But she always had, and that was the problem. Always had, always would. She knew that as surely as she knew that her heart was beating a little faster right now, and that her breaths were slightly quicker. "I, um… It's not easy to blot it out, and sometimes…" Sometimes, what? It just overtook her? How could she tell him that, when he applied everything she said to Max— how he would react, the things he would say, the feelings he would have? It was such a delicate line, and she wasn't the one who should be walking it. Heaven knew, when it came to the emotional journey, she was barely able to take care of herself. So how could she ever do anything for Dermott's little boy?

She wanted to, though. Deep in her heart she wanted to pick him up and hold him and never, ever let anything else bad touch him. No one had done that for her, not even her grandparents, and in the deep, dark hours when she'd slept alone in her bed she'd clung to her dolls, wishing the lifeless stuffing inside them could hug her back. But Max had Dermott to do that, and he would. Of that, she had no doubt. So there really was nothing else to say. "You know, Dermott…I think your hand is all fixed up now. Provided you don't put it through another plaster wall, you should be fine in a few days."

She backed away, took a look at her bandaging job, and nodded. "And make sure you don't do something stupid with your other hand in the meantime."

"Something stupid?"

"Walls, doors, any solid object. The town doctor really does need one hand available to him."

"The town doctor might have to rely on the town nurse for an extra hand for the next few days."

"You know where to find her. She's right upstairs." Scared to death of what might happen when he did find her. And wanting it *so* badly.

Tonight she was especially restless. She'd been holed up in her apartment for hours, reading, pacing the floor, reading some more. A while ago she'd gone to the diner for a light supper, then taken a good, long walk, but once she'd come home the restlessness had begun again. So much so that she needed to get out of there. Needed to go for another walk, or perhaps a good, hard run. Something…anything to take her mind off Dermott, Max…her future here.

After tying on her white athletic shoes, Jenna dashed down the flight of stairs, pausing briefly at Dermott's door, wondering what he and Max were doing inside, wishing that she could be part of it, knowing that she didn't have that right. Then she hurried on down to the first floor and out the front door, but when she made it to the sidewalk and looked back at the building to make sure the door had latched, she noticed a light on in exam one. She couldn't see into the room, of course, but there was a faint glow through the shade, so she went back to turn off the light and discovered Dermott in there, sitting in the dimness.

"Is it your hand?" she asked, her voice almost a whisper.

"Hand's fine," he snapped. "Max thought it was funny that I tripped and broke the wall."

"You lied to him?"

"I protected him. How could I tell him that I got angry and hit the wall? He's an abused kid who has no concept that his dad could ever have a bad temper. So what should I have done? Planted an image in his mind that the one person he trusts most in the world got so angry he hit the wall? Would that somehow remind him of his mother?"

"Max knows what his mother did, Dermott. Even in his young mind, he understands how she was. And he also understands how you are. What happens, though, if in an unguarded moment he sees you react, sees you hit that wall? What then? Does he live in mortal fear of you because he never knew it was in you? Or do you let him know that you do react that way on occasion, but that it has nothing to do with him and never will? He lived in a secret world for a long time. Think about that. He never told anybody what was happening to him... maybe because he was ashamed and thought he deserved the abuse, or maybe because Nancy threatened him. We really don't know yet, but what you don't want to do is force him to go back and live with secrets again. Even if it's your secret."

"It's always going to be a balancing act, isn't it? My need to protect him versus doing the right thing."

"You're a good father. Just start from there and the rest will work itself out." She took several steps closer to Dermott, then studied him for a moment. He was agonizing over the little things and she loved that in him. Never, in her life, had she known anybody who tried so hard to do the right things by everyone the way he did. To the exclusion of himself, actually. Which was a shame. Dermott had become so involved in caring for all the people around him that he'd forgotten about himself. "Is Max upstairs?"

"He's spending the night with his grandparents. Under the circumstances..." he held up his bandaged hand "...we all thought that would be better. And they're going to make popcorn and root-beer floats. I was going to make...boxed cookies and nothing." He laughed. "Never let it be said that my son doesn't know a good thing when he sees it."

Jenna laughed. "Well, then. Since that means you're a bachelor for the evening, do you want to go out and take a run with me? I need to work off some energy, and a couple of kilometers might just do that."

"Run?" Dermott sputtered. "Do you know how long it's been since I've done anything like that?" He shook his head. "Even if I wanted to, I'm so out of practice I'd make it a block or two, then you'd have to carry me back. Maybe I could drive alongside you and watch?"

"Drive? How's that going to be good for you?"

"It's not the driving that's good for me. It's the watching... watching you."

"You're trying to be incorrigible, aren't you?"

He chuckled. "Am I succeeding?"

He was, in so many ways. Which should have made her happy, buoyant, dancing on clouds. But she wasn't, because the happier she was, the more she stood to lose. Happiness was such a risk in her life and it frightened her more than just about anything she could think of. Suddenly, she was sober, sad, depressed. "Look, I'm going for a run. You can come, or you can stay here. Just…just do whatever you want."

A puzzled frown crossed his face when he saw her mood swing so quickly. "What is it, Jenna? What does that to you?"

"I can't do this," she whispered. "Can't talk about it, Dermott."

"Don't you trust me?" Pushing himself up off the chair, he took a few steps toward her, and she took a few steps backward.

"Of course I do. It's just that…" She'd never wanted to settle more than she did now. Better than anyone else, she knew what she had in her, and it always made her leave. A person's true nature had a way of winning even when it was being held down. But, oh, in the dim light of the night, with nobody around except the two of them, she really *didn't* want to run away, and she so much wanted to tell him that. She also wanted to take those few steps forward, into his arms. To stay there forever. Wanted it so badly she could feel it. But she could also feel the fear running through her, cold and brutal. And that's what stopped her, what pulled her back. "Why are you making this so difficult on me, Dermott?" she asked, her voice frail, on the verge of tears. "I've been honest with you, and that's all I have."

"No, it's not, JJ. You don't allow yourself…anything. Don't allow yourself to be honest with yourself. You get so close, then…" He shrugged. "Is it me? Am I reading something into this that's just not there? Or is it about my screwed-up mess of a life?"

Jenna shook her head. "From where I stand, your life looks wonderful. And no, it's not you, Dermott. It's just that…that my life has these patterns that keep repeating themselves. Nothing works out and I move on, start over. I've already told you all that."

"But how would you know that it won't work out if you never stay in one place long enough to find out?" He reached out and ran his hand through her hair. It was tied back for her evening run, and he pulled the clips away, letting it down. "Life doesn't come with guarantees, but that doesn't mean it's always best to just give up on it and go away."

"It does if you hurt other people. And that's what I always do—I hurt other people."

"Have you ever thought that the biggest hurt those other people might suffer is losing you?"

The biggest hurt, or the biggest blessing. The two were interchangeable. "Pretty words, Dermott, but we still can't do this. As much as you want it, and as much as I want it…you know we can't. You both need someone stronger than me. And I'm not strong, Dermott. I go through life being scared…of everything, of everyone."

"Oh, Jenna. You are strong, even if you don't see it. You're the strongest person I've ever known. And if you are scared, that's OK. We all are at some time."

"But other people get over it. I don't."

"Because no one has ever helped you. You're always so busy taking care of other people, but you've never let anyone take care of you. And here we are, both of us scared, both of us playing all the way around our feelings—circling, but never quite landing. What I know more than anything else, JJ, is that if this is something we both want, shouldn't there be a way to have it? To make it be what we want it to be?"

"Ideally, maybe," she admitted.

"So tell me what you want, Jenna. If your deepest hopes and dreams came true, what would you have?"

She spread wide her arms and spun around. "This. All of it." She wanted it like she'd never known she could want anything. Except Dermott. And she wanted him even more. "But what happens if Max gets attached to me and I just can't do this? What if I've overestimated myself? And what happens to you?"

Dermott drew in a stiff breath, held it for a moment, then let it out. "But what happens if you *can* do all this, Jenna? What happens if you allow yourself to have it all?"

"If I allow myself? It's not like I want things to turn out the way they do."

"But don't you predict the outcome before you begin anything? Don't you always have an escape plan ready before you open the door and walk in? I mean, you expect things to turn out badly for you and when they do, you simply accept it as your lot. When your father beat you, he made you believe you deserved it, and you've never stopped believing it. Not in the most profound sense, anyway."

"How can you say that to me, Dermott? Nobody deserves what he did to me."

"No, they don't. But the little girl still inside you doesn't believe that. She's still taking the blame for things she didn't do."

"And things she did do." She turned to leave the room, but stopped short. What he said was right. Here, in this situation, she'd set herself up with so many different escape plans it surprised her. Small-town life too confining, Dermott's son with too many problems, too little work to keep her happy, their past, or even their current relationship getting in the way... there were so many excuses, so many reasons to leave, yet she didn't want to. Dear God, she didn't want to. Which was why she piled excuse on excuse. The more she wanted to stay, the more she had to go. Somewhere in the pile, she'd find the one reason that would work best, the reason that would sever the attachment she'd formed here. "You have a right to dictate my professional life, but that's all you get. All I'm going to give you." And that was another exit excuse.

"Look, Jenna, you accused me of lying to Max, and you

were right. I did. Right or wrong, it's always about protecting him and I'll admit I make mistakes. That was one, and when the time is right I'll set it straight. But what about you? What about the lies you tell yourself. When are you going to set them straight?"

"The one thing I don't do is lie to myself. I've always had a clear picture of who I am and what I can have." She should have been angry, but all the anger had seeped away. Now she was sad—sad for the things in her that Dermott recognized, sad for the thing inside herself that she'd always known. Swiping back a tear, Jenna turned back to the exam-room door, hesitated for a moment, then stepped into the hall, leaving Dermott in there alone. There was nothing else to say. No arguments. No excuses. They were both right and there was no point in prolonging the painful moments between them. As Jenna wandered down the front steps and stopped on the curb outside, though, she wondered if there really was any point in prolonging her stay here. It was always going to be this way—she and Dermott locked in a tug of war where both were always so close to stepping over the line, yet neither of them would win.

Well, he hadn't intended what he'd just done to Jenna. But this wall between them…it was so impenetrable. He wanted to get through it and, if he wasn't mistaken, so did she. Yet he was preoccupied, she was scared. That was a bad combination to get past anything. "Damn," he muttered, shutting off the light and heading for the door. This wasn't the time to fall in love, but he had. He loved Jenna and, in so many ways, he always had. Did she love him back? Well, what he hoped was that she wouldn't be struggling so hard against him if she didn't. Yet she was ready to run again. He could see it, feel it. And if she did…he wasn't a free man. He couldn't go after her.

So what would keep her here? If he came right out and told her he loved her, she'd be gone in the blink of an eye. He was sure of that. If he played it out slowly, then Max stood to get hurt because he was growing attached to Jenna in ways Dermott had never expected. And, yes, he stood to get hurt too, because having her here was just better. Problems and all, he wanted her in every way, and to prolong the agony of her leaving just put off the pain. But what would keep her here? Or, maybe the better question was, could anything keep her here? "Damn," he muttered again, stepping into the hall. How could something that should have been so wonderful go so wrong?

"Dermott?" she whispered from the shadows. "What are we going to do?" She reached out, ran her fingers lightly over his arm.

"Would it make any difference if I had an answer?" He liked her touch, but it frightened him, because he liked it too much. Craved it. Wanted more of it. And everything else that came with it. "Aren't you set on doing what you're going to do, no matter what?" Bitter words maybe, but they were the ones he needed to cling to. And this time it wasn't to protect Max. Right here, right now, he was the one who needed the protection.

"Honestly, I don't know. Because you were right. I do have an escape plan."

The muscle in his jaw clenched. "So what things do I need to say to you, Jenna? What will convince you that you're safe here, that you don't have to run away? Because I sure as hell don't know what to say except that I don't want you to leave, and I'm not sure that's good enough." He turned and went back into the dark exam room, not sure if he wanted to get away from her, or if he wanted her to follow him in. Then he sat on the exam table, and watched her silhouette in the hall. It wasn't moving. Not coming in, not leaving.

Not sure which he wanted her to do.

"Why would you even bother with me, Dermott?" she finally asked, taking a few steps in the door.

"Why wouldn't I, Jenna?" When she finally reached the

exam table, she stepped boldly between his knees and looked up at him. Even in the near-dark, the only light that of the streetlamps streaming in through the slats in the blinds, she was so breathtakingly beautiful. She had been years ago, and the years had only improved her.

"Because you're a smart man, and you can see who I am."

"Yes, I can see." He brushed the back of his hand across her cheek and over her lips. "And what I see is everything I've ever wanted."

Jenna stepped back. Pure instinct. She wanted to run. He knew that. He also knew that she was struggling with herself.

"Dermott, I…" She didn't finish. But she didn't leave, either.

"Make it simple, Jenna."

"How?"

"Why don't you come over here and tell me what it is you are? Tell me all the things you think you are, and I'll show you how you're wrong." He patted the edge of the exam table.

Jenna took a step forward, then hesitated. The outcome couldn't be good, no matter how she framed the fantasy. That she would have no future with Dermott was already etched in stone but, then, so were her growing feelings. How could she have been so careful about resisting, then find herself here, like this?

Because this was Dermott, that's why. But she wanted this, wanted all the feelings flooding through her, wanted to forget every possible angle of common sense and simply have this moment. "Dermott, I shouldn't, but I want to," she said, falling into his open arms.

Dermott received Jenna, and she was a perfect fit in his embrace.

"It's still one day at a time," she whispered, almost shyly. "No promises." But so full of expectations now.

In answer, his arms encircled her, his unbandaged hand taking hold of the stretchy fabric of her shirt. "One day, one

night…right now. It is what it is, and for now, that's enough."
He teased the garment slowly up, kissing every morsel of the
skin he exposed, and the feel of him was so good, Jenna
merely sighed, contented to savor his touch for a moment,
before she arched herself into him, begging more.

"Let me know if I hurt your hand," she whispered.

"What hand?" he growled, taking a painfully, deliciously
long time removing her bra. He tantalized her nipples through
the fabric with a light touch, then planted demanding kisses
above the line of the lace. His patience was surprising, his
ardor restrained, and Jenna gasped over the delight of sensations he caused.

Sensations she wanted, always and forever, only from
Dermott.

Dermott took his time with every one of Jenna's sensitive
spots, some she knew, some she didn't. His search for even more
sent untried jolts of need and desire gushing through her every
time he paused to explore something yet untouched. Fingers
burning into her quivering flesh as they slid across her belly and
pressed beneath her running shorts thrilled her in ways she'd
never been thrilled, moving methodically to pleasure points
with only one purpose—to give up even more thrills.

Wanting nothing to hamper that which aroused her, Jenna
backed away from the exam table and beckoned Dermott down
the hall to his office, where he found her only seconds later,
without her running shorts. She was standing there at the edge
of his sofa, clad only in her panties, waiting for him to come
closer. When he did, she pulled him onto the sofa, then shut her
eyes as he continued his exploration, stopping at her navel and
caressing it with a light kiss. "You're wearing my favorites," he
growled into her belly as his thumb began to inch down her
panties.

"You have favorites?"

"Anything silky and brief on you are my favorites. What
color are they?"

"Blue."

"Got anything in red?" he asked. "You'd look sensational wrapped in red." He pressed a hard kiss below her navel, just above her panty line. "You'd look sensational out of red."

"You look sensational out of anything," she said, reaching up to unbutton his shirt. Once it was off, she went for his jeans, unzipping them, then inching them down slowly until they were stopped by the bulge of his erection. That's when she knew that she either had to run right now, or there would be no turning back. "Dermott, all this..." she whispered.

"Do you want it, Jenna?"

She didn't hesitate for a moment. "Yes, I want it." But she didn't just mean the moment, which was what she was sure Dermott meant. She wanted it all. And it was too late to hide her heart. "I want it," she whispered again, her voice hoarse with desire and love and so many other emotions she was afraid to understand, or admit.

"When you came back, did you lock the front door," he asked, "or should we be prepared for night visitors?"

"I locked it." Because she'd hoped for this. Every last speck and sensation of it.

He dropped to one knee over her, but Jenna rose up and pushed him down on his back, then took her place on top of him.

Dermott shuddered as she raked her fingers over his chest, which made her shudder, too. She loved the feel of the hard lines she stroked along his ribs, loved the way he shuddered when her thumbs taunted his nipples. He sucked in a more explosive shudder when she bent to taunt his nipples with her lips, her tongue, her teeth. He held his breath for a moment before letting it escape, rough and ragged. "It sure would be easier on us if we weren't so good together," he said.

Jenna pushed herself up off his chest for a moment, then said, "But we are good. So tell me how you want me to be good to you, Doctor. For one night, and one night only, following your orders is my fondest wish."

"Meaning?"

"Meaning tell me, Doctor. Tell me now, because tomorrow starts in just a few hours, and I don't know what will happen tomorrow." Meaning, no escape plans in place.

"Then make it coffee," he growled. "I'll take mine black."

"Don't do coffee, Doc."

"Yes," he sighed. "I know. But you and that big coffee pot, that was the first time I was ever aroused by you."

"Was it me, or the coffee you wanted?"

He chuckled. "That day you refused to get Dr. McNichol's coffee set off a whole chain reaction in me that, it seems, hasn't died down yet."

"Well, no coffee right now, but will this do instead?" She stretched her body along his hard lines, matching contour to contour, trying to feel every inch of his body against every inch of hers. In the cocoon again, but without the blanket. This was where she wanted to be.

Dermott moaned lightly as she pressed her knee up over his hip, and she immediately pulled back. "I'm sorry," she gasped. "Did I hurt you? Can I get some ice for your hand?"

"It's not my hand that's hurting right now," he gasped.

"Oh," she choked. "I thought… I mean…"

"You won't hurt me, Jenna," he said, his voice so soft it nearly melted away. "I promise, you won't hurt me."

This might not hurt him, but she so feared it would hurt her in ways she'd never been hurt before. Because, for the first time in her life, she truly loved someone. And, she believed, someone truly loved her.

It was crazy, the way she wanted him, and didn't want him. She knew that. But knowing it and changing it were two different things, just like love and sex were. One didn't necessarily have to go with the other. But as she parted her legs and felt him enter her, there were no interchangeable feelings here. This was love, and everything that went with it. And as they came together in a rapid explosion, their one need so great that there was nothing else in the world for those few moments, tears slid down Jenna's cheeks for all the things she wanted, and was so close to having, yet was afraid to take as her own.

"Jenna?" he whispered, in the waning moments, when they were too spent to move, too satiated and contented to do anything but linger. "Are you crying?"

"Of course I'm not!" she snapped, then sniffled.

Dermott didn't say another word. He merely pulled Jenna closer and held onto her like he'd never held onto another person in his life. And they both lay there together, quiet, and wondering what would happen to them come morning.

In the morning when the sun came up, Jenna was frazzled over getting from the office to her apartment on legs that were still wobbly. "It's late," she gasped, totally shocked that she'd slept so long and so well—a pleasant side effect of falling in love and making love over and over.

"What have I done?" she moaned, making a mad dash for her clothes, which seemed to be scattered everywhere.

Dermott held out her bra, dangled it off the tips of his fingers for her. "Specifically, which time?"

"All night!" she cried, yanking it away from him. He was dressed. At least, the lower half of him was.

"Do you want the medical assessment, or…?" A devilish grin crept to his lips. "A more graphic description?"

"That's not funny, Dermott. Someone could walk in here any minute. Mrs. Ketterman! Today's her day, isn't it? And I don't have her prune Danishes."

"Tell her you had great sex and forgot." He reached out and took hold of Jenna's arm as she was fighting to get her bra fastened. "Just slow down, OK? You've got plenty of time. The prune Danish will wait. And the door's still locked."

All of that was well and good, but Jenna needed a nice cold stream of water to wash some sense into her. What she had done…it was crazy. She'd spent the night with him! In his arms. Making love, loving making love. "What have I done?"

she murmured again, minutes later, as she looked into the mirror before she stepped into her shower. The evidence of Dermott was all over her body, the little places where he'd kissed and nibbled. The evidence of Dermott was so rooted in her heart, too.

She'd made a mess of things even more than they were already messed up. That's what she'd done.

"I can't believe this," she said, tilting her head back to let the water trickle down her face. One night, when she'd intended only an hour, and look what had happened. *Fantastic* was what had happened. Fantastic, wonderful, amazing. "Stupid, Jenna. That's what you've done. Something stupid." She moaned, leaning back against the shower, wondering if she could just disappear down the drain. "OK, I can deal with it. Be adult about it." Adult, calm, noncommittal. Brace herself against the feelings again. But could she work with him? See him every day, want him in so many ways, know what it would be like, and still maintain a professional demeanor?

No. The answer was simple. She could not. She was Jenna Lawson, true to form. "So I'll leave," she said, melancholy mixing with her newfound resolve. "Right now. Make it perfectly clear that this was a mistake of monumental proportions then show myself to the door."

Although watching him sleep, then waking up next to him had been so nice. Curling into Dermott's arms, feeling the beat of his heart against her cheek…all too wonderful, which was why she was in the shower right now, trying desperately to scrub away the remaining vestiges of any romanticism that might have accidentally seeped in and dallied. This was Dermott Callahan, after all. Exquisite. Sexier than any man had a right to be. Just to see him was to want him. Beyond all reason and sensibility, she had wanted more time. But theirs was not a relationship where more was allowed, and she had to reconcile herself to that fact.

* * *

Dermott sat in Jenna's kitchen, listening to the gentle spray of the shower. Right now, she was in there plotting an exit. He knew that. Knew it last night when they'd made love for the third time. Jenna was a woman who wouldn't allow expectations, romance or any hints of something other than a fling, which certainly did keep it simple as far as their relationship was concerned. If that's the way he wanted it to be. But it wasn't, damn it. He didn't want simple any more.

Maybe it was too soon to think in terms of forever, yet maybe it wasn't. But the problem wasn't what he wanted to think. It was Jenna, and how *she* wanted to think. And right now she was taking a nice, long shower, counting the many ways she could run from this. Or deny it. Or turn it into something it was never meant to be.

It did make him angry, actually. Sure, he had other problems in his life. Dealing with Max and his uncertain future was a huge problem. Dealing with all the leftover emotions from his marriage was a problem. But he didn't want to think about those. Didn't want to think about anything other than how he could keep Jenna right here. Teach her to trust. Show her that she didn't have to run any more.

No, he wasn't thinking in terms of that nice little country cottage with the white picket fence, just the three of them making a cozy family. But he wasn't necessarily *not* thinking in terms of it, either. He wanted something other than his work in his life. Something to ground him the way he felt grounded around Jenna. Wanted it bad. He'd known it the very first time he'd seen her—all that fierce determination on her face while she'd marched that huge coffee pot down the hall. All that bravado she exuded when she really wasn't so brave at all. In Jenna's world, everything still had amazing potential. Even though she didn't know it, didn't see it, didn't believe it, that's what everybody saw when they looked at her—an amazing optimism worn right on her sleeve. Along with her heart. That's why she fought so hard for the things she believed in.

But Jenna never backed down. Once she took a stand, that's where she stayed. He feared that hadn't changed in her. She would leave in spite of what she truly wanted, since she believed that anyone who had her in their lives would be hurt by her. Because she was hurt. The truth was, it was just the opposite. Not having Jenna was what would hurt. Which meant that this morning, right now, he needed a clear head seeing how, in a few minutes, when she stepped out of the shower, there would be no softness and vulnerability showing on her. Not one speck of it. Her resolve would be firm and she would do what she thought she had to do.

Unless... A smile slid over Dermott's lips. Could he change her mind before she left the shower? It was certainly worth a try.

Sliding off the kitchen chair, Dermott was out of his jeans and boxers by the time he'd strolled casually to the bathroom door, debating his next move with every step. Would she? Wouldn't she? It was Jenna, so there was no way of telling. "Why not?" he finally said, giving in to his basic need and pushing the door open a crack. They'd had a wonderful time last night, no denying that, so why not turn it into a wonderful morning? Do it, or die trying, he thought as he stripped off his T-shirt and ventured in.

Inside the bathroom, the air hung so thick with the sweltering humidity from the shower spray that the gush of cool breeze from his side of the door caused the shower curtain to flutter open, and that's when he first saw her. As well as he knew her in *that* way, the sight of Jenna naked, in the shower, took his breath away.

"Dermott?" she cried, reaching out to grab a towel that she couldn't quite reach. "What are you doing in here?"

"Watching," he replied, making no attempt to move, or to even avert his stare. "Watching something amazing."

Twisting herself into the transparent shower curtain, Jenna

huffed out, "Could you at least be a gentleman and hand me a towel?"

Without a word, Dermott grabbed a towel from the rod and stepped into the shower with it. "Here's your towel," he said, dropping it to the shower floor, where it rippled around her feet, absorbing the water from the spray.

Jenna looked down at the towel, then up at him. "I thought that after last night…"

"Last night wasn't enough."

"But I have work to catch up on before our first patient comes in. Some charts to finish…"

"So do I." He reached over and outlined a circle around her nipple with his index finger. Beautiful nipple, dark, such a perfect contrast to her soft, pale skin. He liked the way her nipple puckered in the water. Loved the way it puckered to his touch…between his lips. "Important work. Right here. So many medical details that need attending, it seems." He took her hand and guided it to his erection. "Yours and mine."

"This isn't fair," she choked. "You had last night."

"So did you. But can you tell me that you don't want this morning?"

"We can't…"

"Sure we can." Moving his hand from her breast, he traced a line down her belly and stopped just under her belly button. "So here's my quandary. I could quit right now, turn on the cold water, fend off the conspicuous with a good, strong chill then walk away. But what about you?" He inched his hand downward. "Could you quit right now?" And downward. "Take a cold shower?" And downward. "Then walk away?" Sliding his hand over her perfect mound, he stopped just before he reached her pleasure point, that spot he'd found so easily last night, and listened as her breaths went from steady and sure to rapid and shallow. "Should I reach for the bar of soap, Jenna, and finish bathing myself? Or should I reach for you, and finish whatever it is you need finishing?"

"Louse," she hissed, thrusting herself at him. "You really are a louse, you know."

"If you say so."

"I say so," she whispered huskily, raising her left knee to his hip then twining her leg around him.

When he felt her foot brush the back of his thigh, he spun her around until her back was pressed flat to the wall, then he crushed his pelvis hard into her, grinding...grinding...

"Dermott," she gasped, arching to meet him and squeezing her body so close to his that they shared the same breath, the same heartbeat. Even the droplets of water trickling down over them found no room to slip in between their bodies. And just as Jenna was about to reach the brink, Dermott took a step backwards, then looked down into her face and gave her a sexy wink. "We *are* good in more ways than you know, Jenna," he said, then kissed her softly on her lips as he thrust himself deep into her, all hot and tight, under the sultry shower spray

"We are," she whispered.

Much later, Dermott and Jenna slipped limply down the shower wall to the floor, and clung together, the now-cooling water splashing over their bodies in a pure, relaxing elixir. Exhausted from the lust and exalted from the emotions, neither one of them said a word. Instead, they existed, for a short while, in the dreamy euphoria of awakenings that first-time lovers throughout the ages had shared, and from which long-time lovers took comfort. It was only when the hazy awareness of reality intruded on their euphoria in the form of a ringing telephone that they finally parted.

Without a word, Jenna grabbed a dry towel, secured it around herself and was out the bathroom door in a split second. One minute later she was back, the look on her face was pure panic. "It's Max. He's sick!"

CHAPTER TEN

IRENE Allen was pacing back and forth on the front porch, wringing her hands, on the verge of tears. She clearly looked like she hadn't slept a wink all night and Frank didn't look much better. He was inside, sitting on the edge of his recliner chair, staring into space, his hands visibly shaking. He, too, was nearly on the verge of tears.

"What is it?" Dermott cried, running past Irene and straight through the front door, already hating himself for last night, for not being with his son. He knew better, and he'd gone against his better judgment. "Where's Max?"

"In the guest room," Frank said, his voice wobbly. "He's, um…he's not sick. No fever, his stomach's fine. But he was up all night, crying, screaming. We couldn't get him settled down."

"And you didn't call me?" Dermott practically shouted.

"We thought we could settle him down," Irene said from the doorway. "We're always so afraid, Dermott, that something will happen to Max, and you won't let him come here again. And we were just trying to…to help him."

"Go sit down," Jenna said gently, leading the woman to a rocking chair near the door. "I'll have a look at Max, and I'm sure everything will be fine."

"I'll have a look," Dermott grunted, pushing his way around Frank and heading straight to the stairs.

Jenna ran to catch up with him, and put a restraining hand against his chest. "No!" she said, her voice unusually firm. "I'll take a look at him first. You get yourself calmed down, and if I need you I'll call for you."

"He's *my* son."

"Do you want him to see you in this state, Dermott? Your face is red, you're angry. You look like you're ready to shove your other fist through the wall."

Dermott sucked in a sharp breath, then closed his eyes. "Go please, JJ," he finally said, his voice so ragged it broke her heart.

It didn't take another prompt. Jenna grabbed Dermott's medical bag and was up the stairs in a split second. But at Max's door, she didn't merely barge in. She knocked first. "Max," she called. "It's Jenna. Can I come in?"

"Leave me alone!" he shouted. He sounded so much like Dermott when Dermott was being stubborn, trying to shut people out. "Go away. Leave me alone!" It was a shout heard all the way downstairs, because within a second Dermott was thundering up the stairs. But Jenna turned and shook her head at him, effectively stopping him on the landing.

"I thought maybe you'd go and get ice cream with me."

There was a pause, as if he was considering his response. Then, "I haven't had breakfast yet."

"Ever had ice cream for breakfast? You know…a waffle with chocolate syrup, and a scoop of vanilla ice cream on top?" She'd never had it, but it didn't sound half-bad, if you were five. Which her little patient was.

"Chocolate ice cream," he insisted.

Jenna smiled. Max *was* so like his dad. She really loved this kid. "Caramel syrup's good, over *vanilla*."

"Chocolate," he insisted again.

"Just go on in," Dermott whispered.

She shook her head. "He needs some control over his situation," she whispered in return. "Needs to know that his wishes are respected." She motioned him back. "Do you really like chocolate that much, Max?" she called.

Long pause again, then finally… "I like strawberry some. Could I have strawberry on my waffle?"

His voice was closer. Max was just on the other side of the door now. But he wasn't opening it. And she still wasn't going to force him. So she sat down on the floor, and didn't say another word. Not for a full minute, until Max finally did open the door and peek out.

"What are you doing?" he asked.

He was still in his blue pajamas, and he looked like a child who'd had a rough night. His eyes were still red and puffy, his face pale. She really did want to just hold him, pull him into her arms and tell him that everything would be fine, the way she'd wanted someone to do for her when she'd had nightmares. But wisdom and a lot of years of study held her back. "I'm just sitting here, waiting for you. What are you doing?"

He shrugged.

"Are you thinking about waffles?"

"Maybe."

"Good, because that's what I'm thinking about."

"The big guy won't let me eat ice cream for breakfast," he said, his face drawing up into a pout.

"Have you asked him?"

Max shook his head. "Did your dad let you eat ice cream for breakfast?"

Honesty time here. Admitting her life to Dermott was one thing, but to Max? The thing was, she owed this child honesty. He couldn't heal without it. "I didn't get to eat breakfast too much. I had to fix it for my dad, and by the time I got through, I had to go to school."

That caught his attention a little. "Could you have ice cream for lunch?"

"I didn't eat lunch too much, either. We usually didn't

have enough food in the house, and my dad wouldn't give me any money."

"No peanut butter and jelly?"

Jenna shook her head.

"But didn't you get hungry?"

"Sometimes. But sometimes my friends gave me part of their lunch, so it wasn't so bad."

"Your dad was mean," he said. "Just like my…"

Jenna's breath caught in her throat. She knew better than to prompt him into saying something, so she continued. "Yes, he was a mean man. Sometimes he hit me." She glanced at Max to see what his face registered, and there was mild interest there. But not enough to convince her that he was ready to talk about anything. "But I had very nice grandparents, like you do."

"The ones with horses."

"Only they wouldn't let me ride when I was little like you. Only when I was older and went to live with them."

"Did *they* let you have ice cream for breakfast?"

"No. I had to eat things like cereal and toast." Max actually sat down across from her, legs crossed, on his side of the door. It was the boundary, like she had her boundaries, and she understood that.

"Did they fix you lunch, too? Because it wouldn't be good if they were mean like your mommy."

"My daddy," she reminded him.

"Where was your mommy?" he asked.

"She died when I was little."

"Like my mommy."

From behind her, Jenna heard a slight gasp. She chanced a quick look at Dermott, who looked very stressed, and gave him a reassuring smile. "Your grandparents are awfully upset this morning, Max. Did you know that?"

He nodded. "I had a bad dream again."

"About someone you know?"

He nodded, but didn't go on. And she didn't want to press him for details. "But you didn't let them help you? Because I know they would have."

"Not like my daddy. He knows how."

"Sometimes you have to tell other people what you want, Max. If you don't, they won't know. I mean, right now, do you know what I want?"

He shook his head.

"That's because I didn't tell you. But if I told you that I want a puppy, then you'd know."

"A puppy?" That definitely caught his attention. "Me too! Only the big guy says I'm not ready." He thought for a moment, his face changing from a pout to a deep, contemplative frown. "Maybe you could get a puppy, since the big guy can't tell you what to do, and we can pretend that he's my puppy, too."

"Or maybe you can tell the big guy all the reasons why you want a puppy. Want to tell me first? You know, practice?"

Max emitted a deep sigh. "Because I like puppies. They're fun. They like to play ball. And they can sleep with me at night when I'm…"

So close again. Max was one stubborn little boy. He reminded her of herself when she'd been young. Even now, in some ways. "Would you have slept better last night if you'd had a puppy with you?" She really didn't mean to make a case for Dermott getting a dog, but Max did seem to have strong feelings about it.

"If I had a puppy, then I wouldn't have to look at *her*."

"Who, Max? Who did you have to look at?"

He didn't answer. Instead, he drew his knees up to his head and pulled himself into a tight little ball.

"Can I come in, Max? Can I come in and see what you had to look at?"

He didn't look up at her, but he did nod. So Jenna stood, gave Dermott an apprehensive look and stepped around Max.

It was a typical room, done up in browns and blues. There were toys scattered on the floor but, apart from that, nothing set it apart as Max's room. It was simply a guest room, small in space, sparse in furnishing. And nothing in it seemed to be something that should have upset the boy. So Jenna walked over to the closet, took a look inside. Again, nothing. And nothing on the table next to the bed, or the dresser across from it. On a burst of inspiration, she looked under the bed, but except for a pair of Max's shoes, there was nothing. So she was stumped. She'd fully expected to find something in this room that had triggered his nightmare and subsequent outbursts.

Walking over to the bedroom window, she parted the curtains, and stared down to the front yard. That's when she saw it—an eight-by-ten portrait of a woman. It had to be Nancy Callahan because she could see so much of Max in the image—the blonde hair, the same shaped face. The photo was sitting on the roof ledge outside the window. Where Max had put it.

Jenna left it there, and when she turned around, Max's eyes were wide, not so much from fright but from the uncertainty of what would happen next. Would he be in trouble? Would somebody hit him again?

It was all Jenna could do to keep the tears from starting, but she did. She'd lived her pain, reconciled herself to adjustments. This time it was about Max, and the whole reality of what he'd lived through was just on the verge of starting for him. "Why don't you call your daddy Daddy, or Dad?" she asked, impulsively.

Max's bottom lip began trembling, and big, fat tears welled up in his eyes. "Because I was a bad boy."

That didn't make any sense to her, but it didn't have to because it made sense to Max, and it hurt him. She could see that. "But you weren't a bad boy, Max."

He nodded. "I was, too. My mommy told me I was, and

that my daddy would go away if I was bad. So if I didn't tell him I was bad, and pretended he wasn't my daddy, maybe he couldn't go away."

Jenna's heart shattered into pieces for this little boy. She was angry for him, too. And she hurt for him. But she was frightened. Max needed someone more, someone better than her. Except right now it was just the two of them, and he trusted her to help him. She could see it in his eyes. *He trusted her.* Needed her like no one had ever needed her before. And she couldn't let all the pain still bottled up inside her get in the way of what she had to do to take care of Max. "You weren't a bad boy, Max. What she said wasn't right. You were *never* a bad boy. Do you understand that? You were never a bad boy and your daddy was never, *ever* going to go away and leave you. He loves you more than anything in this world and he would never go away. You know how much he loves you, don't you?"

The tears finally spilled down his cheeks, and he nodded. But he stood in place, braving the worst of it by himself, and she knew just how that felt. Dear God, she knew. "When I was little, my daddy would call me a bad girl before he hit me. Sometimes I thought I was, but I wasn't, Max. I was never a bad girl. My daddy was wrong, and what he did to me was wrong."

"Did it hurt?" he asked through his sniffles.

"Yes," she said simply. "It hurt. Just like it hurt you when your mommy hit you. But you weren't a bad boy, Max. You were never a bad boy and she shouldn't have hit you, like my daddy shouldn't have hit me."

"It hurt," he admitted, still fighting bravely against the tears, even though the tears were winning.

"I know, sweetheart," she whispered, as Max crept shyly toward her. One slow step at a time. When he reached her, Jenna was on her knees with open arms. "I know it hurt," she whispered, holding him the way he needed to be held. The way she'd needed to be held. "But we're going to make it better now. I promise, Max. We're going to make it better, and no one will ever hurt you like that again. I promise."

She glanced over at the doorway in time to see Dermott turn away. There was so much pain here, and so much love. And so much of her own heart.

Yet they needed more than her. But Jenna Lawson, always on the run, didn't know how to run away from this. So she sat on the floor and rocked Max until he'd cried himself out, and told him the things he needed to hear…things she'd needed to hear. Then she sent him off to get ready for that ice-cream breakfast, and he insisted he could do it alone. So she went downstairs to face what would be equally as difficult as what she'd just faced.

"He's washing up and getting ready to go for ice cream," she said, looking at Dermott, whose back was to her. He was staring out the window at nothing in particular. Irene and Frank were conspicuously absent from the room.

"What was it?" Dermott asked, his voice jagged. "What caused all this to happen to him?"

"A picture of his mother. I have an idea Frank and Irene left it at Max's bedside so he wouldn't forget her."

He whirled around to face her, and his face was surprisingly devoid of anger. What was there was sadness, and fear. And so much pain that she could feel it. "I told them not to do that," he whispered. "Over and over, I told them not to remind Max about his mother. And I trusted them when they said they wouldn't."

"She was their daughter, Dermott." Jenna walked over to him, but instead of tumbling into his arms the way she wanted to do, she stood tall, right next to him. Shoulders squared, head up, she stared into his eyes. "You have to let them know the truth…the whole truth…or Max will be hurt again. It's time. It's affecting him now, and you can't go on keeping them in the dark if you want them to remain in his life. Or the alternative is to pick him up and run to Costa Rica, and never look back. But that's not what you want to do, is it?"

He didn't flinch. Didn't say a word.

"You heard what he said, didn't you?"

Again, no response.

"He wants to deal with it, Dermott, and he needs you there to help him. He also needs his grandparents, but they have to know what they're helping him through."

"You know, Jenna, if we hadn't…"

"What, Dermott? Spent the night together? If you hadn't sent Max to spend the night with his grandparents? If you hadn't put your fist through a wall, which was why you sent him over there? If you hadn't worked so many hours then you might have seen what was happening to your marriage, or to Max? If *I* hadn't run away that day we were interrupted in the closet you might not have married Nancy, or if you hadn't noticed me that day I marched the coffee pot down the hall then we might never have met…" She swallowed hard. "I've lived a life of regrets, Dermott. That's all I've ever had. And I know how they can destroy you. All the what-ifs… you dwell on them, wonder, drive yourself crazy, and in the end, it doesn't matter. You've made your choices and you have to live with the consequences. If we hadn't spent the night together, Max would have been home and this would have been put off. But it was inevitable. It had to happen sooner or later, and in so many ways it's good that it was sooner, because now that it's in the open, you can—"

"Spare me. OK, Jenna. Just spare me. The town knows what's best. They stay away so I can have more time with Max. My in-laws know what's best by putting photos in Max's room after I asked them not to. And even you know what's best…you, the one with the messed-up life, who runs away from everything. Well, you know what? I don't care what anybody thinks is best for my son. He's *my* son. I'll take care of him any damn way I see fit to and the rest of the world can leave us the hell alone."

Jenna took a step back. If ever there was a time to exit, this was it. Go pack her things, leave town, don't look back. Except she couldn't. *Not this time.* "I knew someone who said pretty much the same thing once, a long time ago. Everybody could leave her the hell alone. And to prove that she meant it, she ran away from the best thing that had ever happened to her. Walked out, didn't look back. Got her wish. But you know what, Dermott? Be careful what you wish for. Being left alone isn't what it's cracked up to be. I've been there pretty much most of my life, except for the few years I lived with my grandparents."

"You walked away from them?" he asked.

"Ran away. Couldn't get out of there fast enough. They were good to me, but I didn't think I deserved good. I was a bad girl. That's why my father beat me. That was his excuse, and it stayed with me. I did everything I could to prove to my grandparents just how right my father had been about me and they were about ready to send me away to boarding school because they could no longer discipline me. But I was a bad girl. I deserved to be sent away."

"So you ran, and you're still running."

Jenna shook her head. "No, I'm not running now. Because you need me, Dermott. And Max needs me. But more than that, *I* need *you*."

"How am I going to get through this, JJ?" he asked, his voice barely above a whisper. "I heard everything Max said, and I almost can't believe…can't believe she did that to him. Suspecting it is one thing, but actually *hearing* it…" He shook his head angrily. "I had all these ambitions. Be the best doctor this town could possibly have, be a good husband, be a great dad. And look at me. I failed at it all."

"You didn't fail, Dermott. You were deceived, and I think you were probably naive in a lot of ways, but you weren't… *aren't*…a failure. And you've got the greatest little boy in the world to prove that."

"Did you ever go back to see your grandparents?"

Jenna shook her head. "I called a few times, left messages. But those bridges were burned years ago. They want nothing to do with me, and I don't blame them. I put them through hell."

"Do they know how you turned out, though? That you're a well-educated nurse?"

"I didn't tell them. What was the point? They tried to help at a time in my life when I needed it, and I didn't want it. And the thing is, I wanted them to fight for me, Dermott. Deep down in my heart, I wanted them to care enough to do a royal battle with me over myself. But they didn't. I suppose it was easier letting me leave. Or maybe they never thought I'd go through with it. I did, though, and look at me now."

"Look at you now…engaged in that royal battle for my son."

"Because he has everything I didn't, and it will heal him, Dermott. Right now his wounds are tiny. Don't get me wrong. Tiny doesn't mean they're not deep, or that they can be ignored. They're there. Yet I get the sense that he's trying to protect you…in his own little-boy way, he doesn't want you hurt by the things that hurt him. That's why he won't call you Daddy." She stepped closer and laid a supportive hand on Dermott's arm, but Dermott pulled her into his arms and held her to his chest. For the first time since she couldn't remember when, she felt safe. Felt like she finally belonged. The funny thing was, it didn't frighten her the way she thought it would if she ever found it. Maybe that's because she was ready to find it. Or because she'd found it with Dermott.

Maybe both.

"Will you stay, Jenna?" he asked. "Maybe now's not the best time to ask, because it will seem like I want you to stay and help with Max. But I want you to stay…for me. *Only for me.* And, yes, I'm being selfish about that."

Jenna laughed. "You may be a lot of things, Dermott Callahan, but selfish is not one of them." She paused for a moment, growing contemplative. "When I came here, I didn't want to stay. I wouldn't even unpack all my clothes because that would mean I had expectations, and throughout my life the only thing I've known of expectations is that they hurt. But deep down I didn't want to leave here. I've armed myself practically every day with reasons to leave, and you've seen that. Even last night, after we... This morning, before you joined me in the shower, I'd decided that was an appropriate goodbye for us. The end of some long, unfinished business."

He sucked in a sharp breath, as if bracing himself for the worst.

"But it's still unfinished, Dermott, and I don't think it ever can be finished between us. I think I fell in love with you a little all those years ago, and I know I fell in love with you all the way that day I saw you in the elevator and decided to come here. In my entire life, it was the first time I wasn't running away *from* something, but running *to* something. And I don't want to leave you. If you'll have me, faults and all."

"That sounds like a marriage proposal," he whispered.

"It could be," she said, amazed by her boldness, amazed that all the vulnerability she'd ever felt, and all the fears of rejection she'd always known had suddenly vanished. "If you want it to be."

"I want it to be," he said, lowering his head to kiss her. But just as their lips met, the pad of quiet feet on the stairs interrupted them, and one very unsure little boy stood there, waiting for his breakfast ice-cream date.

"Well, right now, another man wants me," Jenna said, forcing herself to back away from Dermott. She didn't want to, but this next step was necessary for everyone. "Why don't you go have that talk with Nancy's parents? Then join us for..." She glanced at Max, then smiled. "Chocolate."

"I knew you'd come round," Dermott said, taking hold of her hand. "We Callahan men have a persuasive way about us."

"So do we Lawson women," she said, extending her hand out to Max. Then she smiled. The three of them, hand in hand. One family, meant to be.

* * *

One Year Later

"Come on!" Max practically yelled at them. "Mom! Dad! Hurry up!"

"Your son is very impatient," Dermott said, as he held the car door open for Jenna.

"*My* son is a perfect angel. When he's impatient, he's *your* son." She hesitated before she climbed out. It had been so long, and the few brief conversations she'd had with them this past month so strained. But it was time, and with Dermott's support, she could do this. She could come home. "Why don't we just send him up to the door, and we'll wait here." Her stomach was in knots, her hands shaking.

"Dad!" Max shouted again. He was halfway up the walk now, and not too happy at his parents' slow pace.

"Don't you just love it when he calls me that?" Dermott said, pulling Jenna from the passenger's side.

It had taken a while, and sometimes *big guy* still slipped out, but Max was growing more secure in the people he loved, and who loved him most in the world, and the more that happened, the more he called Dermott Dad. And lately he'd started calling Jenna Mom—a name she loved. "Why did I ever agree to this?" she asked, as Dermott practically dragged her along the paved walk to the front door.

"Because you know it's the right thing to do."

"Yeah, well, the right thing shouldn't be making me so light-headed. I think I'm going to be morning sick again."

"I think you were plenty morning sick a while ago, and this is just an excuse." He patted her still-flat tummy. "And even if it is morning sickness, you're in the hands of a fairly competent doctor."

"Who should have stayed home and tended to his medical practice. And kept his office nurse there with him." People were coming back to the medical practice now, little by little. Most of them anyway. A few still stayed away, thinking it was for the best, and a few, like Alisa Charney, were downright un-forgiving, but overall the situation was better for just about everyone. Everybody was still cautious when it came to Max, which was a good thing and, for the most part, time was heal-ing some very deep wounds…time, patience, and a whole lot of love.

Even Dermott's hurt and anger had mellowed a little, although Jenna knew that it might never completely vanish. But he was dealing with it better. No more punching holes in the wall with his bare fists. And now, seven months married, with the help of a part-time, near retirement-age doctor who'd moved over from Muledeer to help out, and Fort Dyott's new computer guru, Leona Hazelwood, coming in three days a week to help—a sure cure for *her* loneliness—the medical practice was thriv-ing almost as much as the Callahan family was.

"They want to see you, Jenna. Why else would they have finally invited you?"

She let out a heavy breath. "Because they felt obligated. Because it's the right thing. Because they want to tell me, face to face, to leave them alone. That what I did can't be undone."

He held her around the waist with a firm hand. "This will be good. You've helped Max and me, as well as Frank and Irene, and now it's time that we do the same for you."

"You're assuming I want to be helped."

"I love that stubborn streak, I love that stubborn streak."

"What?"

"I'm reminding myself that I love that stubborn streak in you."

"You just wait, Dr. Callahan. Your next child is going to get all my stubbornness, and all yours, too."

He groaned playfully. "I don't suppose there's any chance you're really a very mild-mannered, complacent woman who's been faking her stubbornness all along, is there?"

The front door to the old two-story brick house opened and Jenna sucked in a sharp breath, then let it out slowly. It was her grandfather, and he hadn't changed much. Tall, square shouldered, white hair. He was bending down to talk to Max, who'd run on ahead and banged on the large brass knocker. "Not a chance," she said, as she started, in earnest, down the walkway. By the time she'd stopped behind Max, her grandmother had joined them on the porch.

"Grandmother, Grandfather…this is my husband, Dermott Callahan, and you've already met my son, Max."

"The boy who wants to ride the horse?" her grandfather asked.

"The boy who wants to ride the horse," Jenna said.

"Would it be alright if I take my great-grandson down to the stables?" he asked, his voice sounding as unsure as Jenna felt.

Jenna nodded. "It would be alright."

Asa Lawson held out his hand to Max, who took hold eagerly. And as the two of them headed off to the stables, Jenna stood and watched something she'd never, ever expected to see. "It's good," she whispered to Dermott. Then she turned to her grandmother. "Did you happen to make my favorite sugar cookies? Or buttermilk cake?"

Rather than answering, Amanda Lawson opened her arms to Jenna, and Jenna fell straight into them. "Welcome home, Jenna," her grandmother said.

Home. Jenna Lawson Callahan, who'd never had a home of her own, was finally, truly at home. But it wasn't a brick-and-mortar place. Wasn't a three-story medical building on the main street of Fort Dyott or the little white cottage she and Dermott had moved into on the edge of town. It wasn't the barn that Max had succeeded in painting entirely blue and purple, and it wasn't even a horse ranch that stabled the pony her son was now riding. Home was far, far bigger. And Jenna, at long last, had found her home forever.

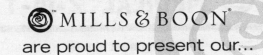

MILLS & BOON®

are proud to present our...

Book of the Month

Expecting Miracle Twins
by Barbara Hannay

Mattie Carey has put her dreams of finding
Mr. Right aside to be her best friend's surrogate.
Then the gorgeous Jake Devlin steps into her life...

Enjoy double the Mills & Boon® Romance
in this great value 2-in-1!

Expecting Miracle Twins by Barbara Hannay and
Claimed: Secret Son by Marion Lennox

Available 4th September 2009

Tell us what you think about
Expecting Miracle Twins
at millsandboon.co.uk/community

MEDICAL™ 2-in-1

Coming next month

ITALIAN DOCTOR, DREAM PROPOSAL
by Margaret McDonagh

Gorgeous but shy Dr Ruth Baxter doesn't do relationships –
until a seductive encounter with her handsome new boss,
Dr Rico Linardi! An encounter that convinces Rico that
he wants Ruth not only as his lover...but his wife!

WANTED: A FATHER FOR HER TWINS
by Emily Forbes

Dr Rosie Jefferson's priority is caring for her orphaned twin
niece and nephew, not her appearance! But deliciously
attractive Dr Nick Masters makes her feel beautiful again and
this single mum finds herself wishing for the impossible...

BRIDE ON THE CHILDREN'S WARD
by Lucy Clark

Years ago, Dr David Montgomery and Eden Caplan shared
a soul-searing kiss. Now, gorgeous doctor David realises
that one kiss wasn't enough – he wants a lifetime,
with Eden as his bride!

MARRIAGE REUNITED: BABY ON THE WAY
by Sharon Archer

The Campbells' marriage fell apart when doctor Liz's gorgeous
firefighter husband Jack thought he couldn't give her the family
she wanted. Now one miraculous night leaves Liz pregnant,
and Jack's determined to be the perfect husband and father.

On sale 2nd October 2009

Available at WHSmith, Tesco, ASDA, Eason and all good bookshops.
For full Mills & Boon range including eBooks visit
www.millsandboon.co.uk

 **MEDICAL**™

Single titles coming next month

THE REBEL OF PENHALLY BAY
by Caroline Anderson

Everyone remembers heartbreaking bad-boy Sam Cavendish
– especially shy practice nurse Gemma Johnson. She's
spent ten long years trying desperately to forget their
secret whirlwind wedding, but Sam's returned to Penhally
and is determined to win back the heart of the only
woman he's ever loved…

MARRYING THE PLAYBOY DOCTOR
by Laura Iding

Seth Taylor appreciates beautiful women, so he can't
wait to get to know his new colleague, paramedic
and single mum Kylie Germaine, better! Only for
the first time ever, Seth's smitten – this eligible bachelor
finds himself wanting to put a ring on Kylie's finger
and become a father to her little boy.

On sale 2nd October 2009

millsandboon.co.uk Community

Join Us!

The Community is the perfect place to meet and chat to kindred spirits who love books and reading as much as you do, but it's also the place to:

- **Get the inside scoop from authors about their latest books**
- **Learn how to write a romance book with advice from our editors**
- **Help us to continue publishing the best in women's fiction**
- **Share your thoughts on the books we publish**
- **Befriend other users**

Forums: Interact with each other as well as authors, editors and a whole host of other users worldwide.

Blogs: Every registered community member has their own blog to tell the world what they're up to and what's on their mind.

Book Challenge: We're aiming to read 5,000 books and have joined forces with The Reading Agency in our inaugural Book Challenge.

Profile Page: Showcase yourself and keep a record of your recent community activity.

Social Networking: We've added buttons at the end of every post to share via digg, Facebook, Google, Yahoo, technorati and de.licio.us.

www.millsandboon.co.uk

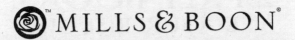

2 FREE BOOKS
AND A SURPRISE GIFT

We would like to take this opportunity to thank you for reading this Mills & Boon® book by offering you the chance to take TWO more specially selected books from the Medical™ series absolutely FREE! We're also making this offer to introduce you to the benefits of the Mills & Boon® Book Club™—

- **FREE home delivery**
- **FREE gifts and competitions**
- **FREE monthly Newsletter**
- **Exclusive Mills & Boon Book Club offers**
- **Books available before they're in the shops**

Accepting these FREE books and gift places you under no obligation to buy, you may cancel at any time, even after receiving your free books. Simply complete your details below and return the entire page to the address below. You don't even need a stamp!

YES Please send me 2 free Medical books and a surprise gift. I understand that unless you hear from me, I will receive 5 superb new stories every month including two 2-in-1 books priced at £4.99 each and a single book priced at £3.19, postage and packing free. I am under no obligation to purchase any books and may cancel my subscription at any time. The free books and gift will be mine to keep in any case.

Ms/Mrs/Miss/Mr _____ Initials _____

Surname _____

Address _____

_____

_____ Postcode _____

Send this whole page to: Mills & Boon Book Club, Free Book Offer, FREEPOST NAT 10298, Richmond, TW9 1BR.